Also by Michael Cadnum

Michael
Cadnum

VIKING

VIKING
Published by the Penguin Group
Penguin Putnam Inc., 375 Hudson Street, New York, New York 10014, U.S.A.
Penguin Books Ltd, 27 Wrights Lane, London W8 5TZ, England
Penguin Books Australia Ltd, Ringwood, Victoria, Australia
Penguin Books Canada Ltd, 10 Alcorn Avenue, Toronto, Ontario, Canada M4V 3B2
Penguin Books (N.Z.) Ltd, 182–190 Wairau Road, Auckland 10, New Zealand

Penguin Books Ltd, Registered Offices: Harmondsworth, Middlesex, England

First published in 1998 by Viking, a member of Penguin Putnam Inc.

1   3   5   7   9   10   8   6   4   2

LIBRARY OF CONGRESS CATALOGING-IN-PUBLICATION DATA
Cadnum, Michael.
Heat / Michael Cadnum.
p.   cm.
Summary: A teenaged diving champion must deal with the aftermath of a diving
accident and her attorney father's remarriage and subsequent arrest for fraud.
ISBN 0-670-87886-3
[1. Diving—Fiction.   2. Accidents—Fiction.   3. Fathers and daughters—Fiction.
4. Remarriage—Fiction.   5. Stealing—Fiction.]   I. Title.
PZ7.C11724He   1998   [Fic]—dc21   97-40938   CIP   AC

Printed in U.S.A.

Set in Palatino

for Sherina

This morning the fish
swim into
the shadow of my hand

CHAPTER

ONE

Someone was saying my name.

I opened one eye and couldn't focus. Light—I could see light. And shapes—human figures. I opened the other eye and blinked, a big effort, like opening and shutting a very heavy garage door.

"She's still not breathing."

It was Miss P's voice. Her words made perfect sense now—someone couldn't breathe. Sunlight slanted through a huge, empty place, an abandoned arena with rows of empty seats. My head shifted to one side. High above the loftiest row of seats a green EXIT caught my gaze and held it. People kept getting in the way, tense onlookers, staring in my direction.

I wanted to tell everyone that I was all right. If I wasn't breathing why wasn't I gasping and thrashing—flopping, like a fish? Why was I blinking my eyes peacefully if there was such an emergency?

Why wasn't I afraid?

Okay, I couldn't breathe. I was lying in a lukewarm puddle,

1

pool water, the smell of chlorine all around. I would say something to make them all feel better in a moment, I promised myself. I would lift my hand, crook my knees.

Miss P turned my head and her fingers worked into my mouth, following the instructions she had taught us but which we had never had to use. *Check for obstructions.* She took a deep breath. The pleasant warm flavor on my lips was the wild-cherry-flavored lip balm Miss P used, a nervous habit wherever she went, using up tubes of the stuff. I made a gagging sound.

I struggled to sit up, but hands forced me back. I took a ragged gulp of air. A loud, breathy howl, in and out. Air was shrieking in and out of me, and I couldn't get enough.

I coughed hard, and I inhaled again, an ugly noise. "Good, Bonnie, you're doing fine," said Miss P.

I let myself relax back down again to the concrete surface. I was doing fine. I felt uneasily pleased at the compliment, even though I knew. I knew this was a kind of lie, the sort of thing you say when someone isn't doing so well.

Jesus, what happened? A metal door wrenched open and footsteps approached, *slap slap slap*, fast, to where I was lying, my hands outstretched. The concrete was hard under my elbows, and the swimming pool sloshed in the distance, the filter valves gurgling. I drew breath and exhaled, just to show I could keep this up.

"Bonnie, everything's going to be all right," said another familiar voice, panting, bending over me. "I called 911," Denise added in a different tone, addressing the onlookers. Then, as though I couldn't hear, "I thought she was dead."

Denise looked odd, as people do when you see them sideways or upside down, her eyebrows underneath her eyes, her tight bathing cap giving her forehead a long wrinkle, one of the reasons I hate wearing one.

Miss Petrossian's eyes peered down into me. I felt naked. A swimsuit isn't much more than a second skin, no extra padding, nothing. I opened my mouth to speak and my body jerked, a shocking spasm, like when you drift asleep and wake with a start. I felt my head roll to one side, independent of my will, a large, bony jack-o'-lantern. Warm fluid spilled from my lips.

"That's good!" said Miss Petrossian.

This was probably the first time I had ever been praised for throwing up. My embarrassment sharpened, but I couldn't help thinking, *Hey, it was easy.*

"Don't move," Miss Petrossian was saying. I struggled, but Miss P held me down again. "Don't," she insisted. I struggled, knocking her arms away with my hands. I sat upright. I was one of those dolls you can snap into different positions, but always dummylike, fake.

"You had an accident," Miss P was saying, her hands on my shoulders so I couldn't climb to my feet. My swimsuit was clammy on me now, a ridge digging into my spine where the straps crisscrossed.

Accident—I associated the word with cars, fender-benders,

bad traffic. And with toilet training. I remembered my mother hating it when a friend's toddler had an "accident" in the car. I gave Denise a look, asking her without talking. "You hit your head," she said.

I must have over-rotated entering the water. I did a reverse two-and-a-half somersault, and screwed up on the rip, the entry. The judges would have scored me 4.0 or 4.5 at best, a really bad score, despite a respectable difficulty factor.

No judges today, though. This was training, rep after rep.

I do it every day.

The near silence was wonderful but spooky, the soft slopping sound a pool makes when it breaks over the edge of the pool, guttering in the filter valves. "You were practicing your tucks," Miss P said. "You hit your head on the platform."

I tried to play it through my own mental video, how I was on maybe my twentieth dive of the day, leaping, stretching out. I couldn't remember it.

Fractured skull, I thought. A hematoma in my brain, far from the centers of speech and memory, but close to where the nerves from the spine secrete themselves in the skull.

My swimsuit was icy, everyone standing too close. I hate constriction and never wear goggles, even for laps, preferring bloodshot eyes to the sensation of a strap around my head.

I wanted to call out for everyone to back off, give me some room. It was only Denise and Miss P and a few others, the spring-board divers, and a few wannabes, people in gym shorts. Just a few tanned loiterers and the guy with the video camera, one of Miss P's assistants.

I worked the puzzle logically. This wasn't the quarter finals—there weren't enough people here. This wasn't the invitationals. We must have been practicing, a routine weekday afternoon. I reassured myself that I might throw up again—it was something I knew I could do.

When men in Day-Glo yellow raincoats and black rubber boots swung through the metal door I didn't associate them with me. There must be a blaze somewhere, I thought, being patient with Miss P, giving her a grateful smile. She pressed a rolled-up towel against the back of my head hurting something back there, a gash.

A woman in a yellow plastic vest stenciled OFD swung a suitcase down beside me. She unfastened a strap. She got a red tank out of the canvas bag, the white-lettered 0_2 Pack sagging inward, the taste of rubber filling my mouth, and an empty, neutral wind, not at all refreshing or pleasant. I shook my head, but she pressed in with the rubber mask. I had seen athletes on TV sucking oxygen like it was pure, crisp mountain air, and here it was just so much neutral gas. *I can quit diving. I don't have to do it anymore.*

I put the thought out of my head. Miss P was giving the paramedics a rundown, pointing up at the ten-meter platform. And I could see the emergency crew gawk up at the platform, thirty-three feet up, stainless steel rails gleaming, and then look down at me. I felt a little pride mixed in with my self-consciousness. I could see in their eyes that they wouldn't like to take flight off a diving platform taller than a third-story balcony.

I put my fingers to my forehead. I was a mess, blood all over my front, only you couldn't see it against the black nylon-and-Lycra-blend swimsuit. I was going to have some awful injury, a big shaved place on my head, and bruising. Or worse. My face would be blue and swollen when my dad got back from his honeymoon in Maui. His new wife, a person I had never actually met, would look at me and feel that she had to be especially kind, and stifle her shock—she had not heard that I was disfigured.

CHAPTER

TWO

"I can walk," I protested. They cinched me tight into the stretcher with three gray straps that squeezed me into sections.

"We're going to roll you along outside," said the O$_2$ Pack woman, and that's just what they did, and if anything made me feel queasy it was rolling so fast, watching the odd light the Olympic-size pool gives to the place, muted glitter on the walls.

Sunlight, and the freshness of outdoors, juniper leaves and wet grass, a sprinkler chattering far away. "They're just worried about lawsuits," said Miss P, running to keep up. "If you get up and fall and—hurt yourself." If you fall and crack your head again, she nearly said.

She was aware that I knew all about legal proceedings, my dad being a lawyer who sued companies for constructing buildings that fell apart. But I could hear the lie in her voice, pretending I wasn't really badly hurt. We both knew that you don't let a concussed individual get up and walk around. They were rushing things as it was, transporting me in a stretcher—

you were supposed to use cold compresses and let the victim lie still.

The Lloyd-Fairhill Academy campus was summer-quiet, a few seagulls settling on the eaves of the computer lab. One of the janitors, good-looking, with dark glasses and a mustache, watched me go by. My hair was sticky with blood, and the stuff was drying on my face—I could feel it like an avocado-and-yucca-butter facial clay left on too long. They jostled me up the stairs to the main street and huffed along, not in very good shape for a crew that was supposed to keep people from dying.

"This isn't necessary," I said, feeling a little sorry for them—they should watch their fat intake and ease off on the Twinkies.

I felt the antiseptic pad under my head growing sodden, and the words came out weak.

When an ambulance screams past you on the street you think: How exciting, or frightening, or reassuring it must be to occupy such a vehicle, traffic jerking this way and that, getting out of the way. You imagine the ride having an emotional rush, chilling or heartwarming.

But it's disorienting. You lie on your back and the electronic *weep weep* of the siren sounds like a warning that has nothing to do with you or your future. I lay there strapped in, trying to figure out where we were by the shifting shadows on the ceiling, down Lincoln Avenue, up past the doughnut shop on Fruitvale, guessing. I only knew for sure when I felt the long whine of the engine as it accelerated up the on ramp onto 580.

You start a dive by making yourself as tall as possible, giving your body the optimum centrifugal force, and then you want to curl as tight as you can, spinning. I could not remember it. I could not remember the fall, toppling out of sync, my body not a projectile any more, not graceful, no magic in it at all, tumbling. I must have fallen in sideways, and Miss P must have hauled me off the bottom of the pool.

A gentle hand wiped the dried soup off my face. "Let's sit you up," said the doctor after shining a light into my eyes, the inside of my eyeballs illuminated, caverns of black and red veins. The cushioned table was covered with white, crinkly paper that crumpled even more every time I shifted.

The doctor used a pair of scissors. I keep my hair short, pulled back and fastened with a bolo band. He worked the band out of my hair, and I heard the whisper of the refuse-bin door as he disposed of the crusty thong. The scissors made a bright, loud *snip snip,* right up against the bone of my skull. I let him attend the back of my head with the sort of bowed head and stubborn patience I associate with a dog at an animal hospital, hating every moment but surrendering to the unfathomable wisdom of his masters.

I was wearing a ridiculous hospital gown, with the back gaping, a towel over my shoulders. "This is very nice," said the doctor, exactly the way a teacher compliments a student in freehand drawing. "Scalp wounds are so often not as bad as they look."

He was older than I expected, tufts of white hair at his temples, not one of the new interns who practice how to be doctors, probing livers for .38 slugs.

"I'm not bad at sewing up heads," he said with a smile almost as good as my dad's, warm, kind, twinkly. He produced a small electric razor from the pocket of his white coat. He caught the look in my eyes and said, "I need to trim just a wee bit more." He sprinkled a few stiff curls he had already snipped into my hand, to reassure me.

My dad's new wife would take one look at me and figure I had ringworm. I had seen Cindy at a distance, getting out of her car, waiting for an elevator, a briefcase under each arm bulging with paperwork. She was pretty, in a quick, bright-eyed way. I didn't want to disappoint my father and show up with mange, and when I competed in Sacramento I'd have to wear a bathing cap so the judges wouldn't nudge each other and whisper, "What's the matter with her head?"

He flicked on the little gray razor and the buzzing resonated throughout my body.

"It's only blood, though," I said, trying to sound confident.

"Don't worry, Bonnie. There isn't any cranial fluid leaking out." He said *cranial fluid* with a little extra emphasis, one of those older guys who talk to teenage girls like they are objects of amusement.

My mother didn't drive nearly as well as she thought she did, and I dreaded the thought of her careening down from upper

Broadway. I asked when I could go home, but he wasn't listening, finished with clearing a patch around my cut. A small clearing, a meadow no bigger than two fingers wide, as I discovered when I felt up across my head, gingerly, carefully. He plucked my fingers away with a little laugh of impatience.

The trash bin in the corner was labeled BIO-HAZARD, red letters. An icy spray misted the back of my head, and then I felt creepy little tugs, minute tightening pinches as he sutured my scalp.

"I'm training for the Cal Expo Invitational," I said. "Next week." The actual water-sports season runs late winter through spring, but there were plenty of exhibitions to keep us busy.

"Next week," he echoed, only half listening.

I couldn't tell him that the academy had the only swimming/diving team in Alameda County invited to the competition. I couldn't tell him that I had begun to have fantasies, Goodwill Games, Olympic trials. My seventeenth birthday was in three weeks, and when she was my age my mother had held a state record for the women's hundred-meter freestyle.

"My wife and I love watching gymnastics," he said.

"I'm a diver," I said, trying not to sound annoyed. One thing I always make clear is how I disdain gymnastics, how little skill and courage it takes to prance the parallel bars compared with the elegance and mental clarity of the dive. Still, it didn't seem right to get smart with a man sewing up my head.

"Of course you are, a diver," he said, a man humoring a precocious child. "We'll have a neurologist do a workup a little later on," he said. "I have two sons," he said, stepping back to examine me from distance with the look a sculptor gives clay. "I always wished I'd had a daughter," he added. It is almost embarrassing the way adults confide in me. I wonder why, and Rowan tells me I have *that look,* someone they can talk to.

"There might be some discomfort," he said.

When I practice medicine, I will say *pain* when that's what I mean.

"I'll see you get medication," he said, and I did feel a stab of compassion for him, a kind man, spending his nights watching Olympic highlights on video. As the daughterless doctor made his way outside, he whisked aside a curtain, a magician who was gradually getting a feel for his act.

My mother blinked against the sight of me perched there on the examination table, but then got her strength together and hurried to my side. But her hug stopped halfway; she didn't want to risk crushing the delicate eggshell of my head. She took one of my arms instead, squeezing it hard.

She said it would be all right, and her voice was tight with emotion. "Who's minding the shop?" I said, using a paper tissue on my eyes.

People love working for Mom, and she has a crew of efficient, self-effacing plant lovers. Mom's exotic flowers end up in *Architectural Digest,* on Mr. Mel Gibson's coffee table. Mom was wearing a green coat much like the one the doctor had been wearing, except that it looked good on her, tucked in at the waist. A yellow, custom-stitched *Green Heaven* decorated her breast pocket.

"They want to keep you overnight," she said.

Paralysis, I thought. I heard myself say that there was nothing wrong with me.

"A nice private room," she said.

CHAPTER

THREE

A knock at the door, and another visitor was in my private room.

"Bonnie Chamberlain," said a slim woman. *Tell the patient her name—that'll make her feel better.* "I'm Dr. Breen." She had short dark hair done in stylish waves, one of those brisk, practical hairstyles that lets everyone know it cost money.

She carried an oversize manila folder with a metal strap to keep the pages from falling out, and a very large peat-green folder, the color of one of my Mom's favorite sweaters. I had been in the hospital two and a half hours and already my files were getting fat. She wore a white medical coat, with a bright yellow scarf at her throat, the sort older women tie in place to hide what Denise calls chicken neck.

"Tell me what happened," she said. She had long, cinnamon-red fingernails, not someone who worked with her hands.

Mom was gone, off making phone calls. Miss P and Denise had slipped away, home for supper, getting on with their lives. I used to imagine hospitals were places people went to get rest.

The doctor took the cap off her pen. For a private room, the place was noisy, plumbing squealing. "Hey, hey, hey," said a relaxed jovial voice somewhere in the corridor, and another voice responded casually, "I know it."

"I already explained everything to the radiologist," I said. The X-ray doctor had been a large woman with thin little legs, hurrying back into her cubicle: "Don't move while I count three."

"But you and I haven't had a chance to talk, have we?" A speck of white on her tongue, a breath mint.

"You're the neurologist," I said, actually just checking. She could have been a journalist, an award-winner. I didn't have a head *ache* so much as skull awareness, a throb in the bone.

How can smiles say so much: I'm in a hurry, stop stalling. Yes, I'm the expert on the human nervous system.

I couldn't stop myself from asking, "Did you look at my X rays?"

"I have them here," she said, nestling the green folder close to her body. "They aren't so hard to examine, if you put them up to the window. Would you like to see?"

I felt like a person being interviewed for an important, long-sought position. I should think before each answer, I warned myself. She would not want to exhibit an X ray unless it proved something.

I didn't want to look.

She put a large transparent rectangle up against the view and held it as she spoke. The process of having my head X-rayed and having the electrical function of my brain measured had taken place on one of the lower floors of the hospital, and at any other time in my life I would have taken an avid interest in the proceedings.

I told myself that I was not appalled at the vision of my milk-white bone, transparent all the way along the skull to the hard wall, where she had trouble indicating the point of impact. "Right there," she said, as the transparency slipped.

Merritt Hospital has views of the Oakland Hills. If I shifted all the way over to one side of the bed, I could almost see the Lloyd-Fairhill campus, a school Mom and I had chosen because the head life-sciences teacher was a former assistant editor for *Science.* And because they had a new, earthquake-proof gym, and had a swim and dive team that competed up and down the West Coast.

Afternoon shadows crept up the slopes and valleys of the hills, filling in the rough sparseness that was still easy to see, where several years before, the great fire had annihilated eight hundred homes.

"No fracture," I said.

"And no detectable swelling," she said, with a wrinkle of amusement appearing on one cheek.

"You mean I wouldn't be sitting here like this if I had a fractured skull."

She had trouble getting the X ray back in its folder. "You should lie back quietly," she said. "And stay calm."

"I'm calm."

"Tell me where you are," she said.

I toyed with the idea of pretending this was a joke. "You check to see if my brain works by giving me a test."

"A little bit like school," she said.

"You're going to give me a chemistry midterm?" I said, staying polite, barely.

"How many elements can you name?"

"In alphabetical order, or by atomic weight?"

When I get to be a doctor I'll remember times like this, I told myself. An after-hours silk blouse peeked out the front of her white coat. She sported sexy black half-heels open at the toe, pedicure and manicure matching color. I rattled off the elements, actinium and aluminum all the way toward zinc and zirconium, but she lifted her hand at californium, not one quarter of the way through.

I named the hospital, told her it was by Highway 580 in an area known as Pill Hill, and that my dad had used several doctors from the hospital as expert witnesses over the years.

"What did you have for breakfast this morning," she said, not giving it the intonation of a question, in a hurry to go to a reception or maybe she had a dinner date with a surgeon. Imagine the cocktail gossip: One of my patients is missing three quarters of her brain.

Dad had always stressed the difference between being a sworn witness and just answering questions. "Ask anybody who was there," I responded. "They got a good look."

"Do you remember?" she asked after a pause.

"I always have the same thing for breakfast," I said, keeping my voice steady. "I mix Trader Joe's Milk & Egg Protein Powder in a blender, and have that with a banana and some toast."

"How did you get to the pool today?"

I kept myself from telling a lie. "I can walk there from home."

"What did you do *today*?" she asked, emphasizing the last word. An attorney would say that she was badgering the witness. But I was being unresponsive, and we both knew it. The hospital sheets are stamped along the seam, Bay Hospital Supply. I ran my hand over the bedding.

"That's what I did," I said meeting her gaze again, my voice suddenly taking on a weight of surprise and sincerity. "That Harlequin Great Dane was out of its yard. A gigantic dog—it scares all the little kids. I talked to it and gave it a pat." My voice dwindled in wonderment: I *could* remember.

The morning came back to me, the thin, gray-haired man creaking by on a bike, delivering throwaway newspapers, a gardener's canvas cloth spread out on the sidewalk, filling with milkweed and cockleburs. The dog stood on its hind legs, front paws on the top of the wall. I had to reach up to pat the dog's head.

I usually get dog saliva on my fingers. It's a little disgusting, but the dog can't help it.

"Tell me," she was saying, "about your accident."

"You do the same thing, over and over. Do the right thing, in the right way, a million times."

"What went wrong?"

Every time a step whispered in the hall I prayed it was Mom, but shadows fled back and forth and the door stayed still.

"I can't remember the dive," I said at last.

Mom was at the window, gazing out through the venetian blinds at the lights of the hills. "We'll have to see how things go," she said, not turning to look at me.

Mom is a striking-looking woman, although I don't know if a stranger would call her beautiful. I find myself looking at her sometimes, just to watch her. She has prematurely gray hair that she wears full, down to her shoulders, and she is tall enough to look good in anything she wears. She has tiny acne scars in her complexion, and when she forgets to put on her makeup you can see her feelings through their disguise.

"There's nothing wrong with me," I said. I had swallowed two codeine tablets. I wondered if they were taking effect. Maybe that was why my tongue felt fat, *nothing wrong* getting stuck, those two *ng* sounds like chewing gum.

Miss P called. I told her this was the first time I had drunk an entire cup of Brim instant decaffeinated coffee. It came with the dinner, and I didn't see how people could drink the stuff.

Denise called, too. She said my voice sounded peculiar but at least I could talk. Denise and I used to go to the same elementary school. Her dad bought her large, hand-crafted dollhouses at a store on Solano Avenue. Long after we had outgrown dollhouses Denise would have me over to help furnish her latest three-story Victorian mansion. I think Denise took up competition diving because we were used to doing things together.

My sister Georgia called while I was getting a little drowsy, and the sound of her voice made me sit up in bed. Georgia never calls anyone, rarely writes, and almost never visits, but not because we hate each other. She's married and lives near Eureka, up near the Oregon border. She and Mom get along fine, communicating through mental telepathy or dream imagery or some other nonverbal technique. I have the feeling Mom worries about me, but feels that Georgia is going to live to be the first two-hundred-year-old human being.

I told Georgia that it was a mistake to keep me here overnight, and I could hear the concern fade from her voice and a familiar, humorous skepticism take its place. Or maybe it was just the difference in our ages.

"What I want to know is," said Georgia, "did you crack the bottom of the pool?"

Rowan called. I bunched the front of my hospital gown together, thankful he couldn't see me. I heard myself chattering, asking him where he was, what he was doing, and he said, with cheerful mystery, that he and his dad were "out in the field."

I heard the crash and lull of surf and wondered what the Beal family project was on this particular night—the sea lion, the kit fox, or some virtually unknown creature whose cry no one had ever recorded before.

"Don't worry," said Rowan.

"I won't!" I responded, despising myself for sounding so

featherbrained. Rowan's usual friends had always been seniors with sports cars, the kind of student Yale sends advisors out to interview. Recently Rowan and I had begun to spend time together, and I still couldn't believe my good fortune.

"They'll have you out of there in no time," said Rowan.

"I know it," I said, as though the brain and everything about it was no mystery to me.

All night I was afraid to fall asleep.

CHAPTER FOUR

The world looked like something thrown together in the dark.

A man on a roof garden in the distance set out a white table and white chairs. They were heavy; he had to drag them into place. When he was done he stood and looked at the sunrise, hands on his hips, like the sun was barely on time.

The sounds of orderlies and nurses saying good morning made me dress quickly, a plaid blouse I never wore, with mother-of-pearl snap buttons, and tight stretch pants, the kind that look like black leotards. Mom had brought the clothes the evening before, and I wondered what she thought of what I usually wear.

The room had an almost perfectly square mirror framed in stainless steel. My face looked back at me, gray eyes. From the front I couldn't see the bite taken out of my head. Even when I turned my head, I couldn't make out the rat bite in my scalp.

Dr. Breen made her one-knock entrance, wearing dove-gray pants and another scarf, silver-blue silk, and something expensive under her white coat—russets and port blues.

"How was your night?" she asked.

"Good," I said. Even when I had slipped into sleep, nurses had awakened me, in and out of the room all night, making sure I knew where the call button was, "If you need to tinkle."

I felt like my skull was floating in midair, but I was sure if I said so Dr. Breen would send me downstairs to have my head fastened securely. The bed had a little wing, like a desktop, that swung into place if the patient wanted to eat or rest her elbows. The wing had locked into place, and I had been forced to squirm my way out of the sheets.

"If you can wrestle one of our world-champion beds," said Dr. Breen, "you can't be doing too badly."

"It's policy," said the orderly. "I know you can walk, you know it. But policy says I wheel you down to the lobby." It was a chrome wheelchair, thin gray rubber wheels. There was a traffic jam—gurneys, wheelchairs, piles of laundry. The orderly pushing me said, "Beep beep," and another one said, "Beep yourself."

"*I'll* tell Dad about my accident," I said as Mom drove down the Fruitvale Avenue off-ramp. I meant: Don't you tell him.

Mom made one of her nonlaughs, not *ha* so much as *puh*. Meaning: I wouldn't dream of interrupting his honeymoon. Although the idea must have had its appeal. Mom preferred to communicate with Dad through her attorney, a long-legged woman who looked like Bugs Bunny without the ears. Still,

Mom was probably tempted by the idea of calling Dad away from bodysurfing to let him know his daughter was expected to live.

The living room looked unfamiliar, as though I had been gone for months. I felt like a prospective buyer: *My, all this space.* It's the color scheme, pale as possible. Mom never uses the fireplace. It's painted white, too, inside and out, even the andirons—Baroque white, the most expensive latex on the market.

The house was populated with cherry-colored heliconias in the dining room, and slick green monstera in the hall. On the landing of the stairs there was a broad-leafed philodendron that looked like a meat-eater. It always left a drool of water on my arm as I brushed by.

"Myrna tried to climb inside my dresser," Mom was saying, "and she tried Grandma's old cedar chest, and she tried the garage."

"It's a miracle she knows what to do," I said.

"She doesn't," said Mom.

Myrna's mother, Katie, had given birth to Myrna's litter in a drawer full of screwdrivers and rusty nails, and my mom's family had once kept a cat who gave birth on the engine of a Chrysler. Grandpa had been experiencing a bad oil leak in the car and had a habit of checking the dipstick, or a terrible thing could have happened.

———

I was just in time. Myrna was in my bedroom closet, in a box Mom had put in among the sandals and worn-through running shoes. Myrna looked up at me as I made the little tsk tsk noises my family makes at cats. Even my dad does it—a habit he kept from his marriage with Mom. Our family never calls "kitty kitty" or whistles or calls a name. We make the crisp sound people make with their tongues against their teeth, the sound that usually means shame, shame.

Myrna usually rose up to meet my touch, a calico cat with tobacco-gold and brunette patches and a white underbelly. Now she arched her back, radiant with whatever feline hormones rush through a cat when she goes into labor. This was her first litter, and she put a forepaw against the side of the sagging Green Giant creamed corn box, bracing herself.

Pink cat water blotted the towel at the bottom of the box. Mom says cats are dumb as doorstops, but she is the one to give Myrna chicken liver. Myrna's flanks heaved. I murmured encouragement, wondering what reassurance she could possibly derive from a member of an entirely different species telling her everything was okay. Myrna made what sounded like a song, or a mating moan. And then she would relax, purring so loudly you could hear it all the way across the room.

I told myself I felt good, and I did, but a ringing in my ears made me sit at the edge of my bed. I talked to Myrna from where I sat, and she made a gentle trilling noise through her nose.

Audrey was asleep in her cage, a white hump almost entirely

covered by cedar chips. Rowan had rescued her from a snake wholesaler, the subject of a video his dad had made. Audrey was a female white mouse and had been scheduled to be a python's lunch. Every time I came home I checked to make sure Myrna had left the mouse alone.

Newspaper articles about Dad decorated my bulletin board along with my Wild Creatures of Africa calendar and pictures I had photocopied from books, the 1912 Olympics, the first year women divers had competed. The black-and-white divers— gray and light gray—smiled out at our world, carefully posed photographs. Even the photo of Sarah "Fanny" Durak, the best swimmer of her era, was a shot the cameraman had arranged with care, the swimmer pretending to be about to leap from poolside in her cap and boxy bathing suit. She had scandalized the world by wearing a one-piece—before then, women swam in a kind of skirted, layered outfit. The only action photo from that period was a blur, an unnamed diver in what looked like a simple forward-dive tuck, her momentum and the early photographic equipment turning her into a ghost.

"Record Award in Cracked Foundation Suit" was tacked to the board beside "Out of Court Settle in Landslide," a headline I had never thought made as much sense as it should. If a house tumbled downhill in record rains, or a cellar filled with long-stored fuel oil, Dad was there to help the owners get what they deserved.

One celebrated case was featured in the most time-yellowed of the articles, Dad standing with his hands on his hips, his suit jacket hanging over one arm. His hair was longer then, mussed by the wind. He was always unknotting his tie, rolling up his sleeves, or putting more clothes on, whatever he could to keep going. "Harvey Chamberlain surveys lead-poisoned land," read the caption. Kids had been playing in the dirt for generations. Dad sued the oil company that owned the land, and dozens of families shared the multi-million-dollar settlement.

It had been so sudden, Dad announcing that he was marrying his secretary, that he would be back in ten days, say hi to my mother. Even Mom, always ready to make some ironic noise or shake her head like she was in on another one of life's jokes, was quiet for a long time. And when she spoke about it at all, it was to say, "He's *marrying* her," in disbelief.

Everyone talks about new life, how precious it is, but sometimes I wonder. The first kitten looked like a dark sock soaked in snot. Myrna got to work, washing, preening away the umbilical thread.

I found myself sitting with my head crooked to one side, making sure nothing fell out.

CHAPTER

FIVE

That night I had the dream for the first time.

Bleach-flavored water invaded my sinuses, my throat. A hammer blow deafened me. I felt my weight lumber awkwardly, falling through the water onto the trowel swirls of the bottom of the pool.

I woke. I kicked at the sheets. It was one of those dreams when you wake thinking, I've been screaming. But you haven't; the dream takes your voice.

I pulled myself out of bed and sat at my desk and turned on the desk lamp. It's so abrupt sometimes, the transition from dark to light. I peeked into the closet, and Myrna blinked upward in greeting, six furry tadpoles nursing.

Audrey is always up at night, running in her well-oiled exercise wheel or nosing around the perimeter of her cedar, searching the wood shavings. She put her snout up to my finger through the rungs, and her whiskers tickled. I let Audrey out of her cage, and she policed my desk top, the lucky dice Dad had given me, and the Silky Sullivan key ring shaped like a four-leaf clover. Mom says I keep everything, and it's true that the bottom drawer of my dresser is crammed with junior high school history tests with *100%* scrawled beside my name, and pictures I've drawn, horses and swan dives.

I had a headache, like a heart inside my skull, rhythmic, vivid red on and off when I closed my eyes.

That morning, before breakfast, I slipped into my swimsuit, black with a Speedo emblem on the right hip. My mother watched, pretending there was nothing unusual happening, while I padded out to the backyard pool and took the steps into the shallow end.

"Are you okay?" Mom asked, keeping her place in a soil catalog with one finger. She buys the stuff from Costa Rica and has to have it irradiated before it ships, and inspected by the Department of Agriculture. She was draped in a dark green velour robe, a large, plush garment.

I gave her an opened-handed gesture: No big deal. The water edged upward, higher on the inside of my thighs. I tried to con myself into thinking I wasn't nervous.

She watched from the edge of the pool. She had just completed her morning swim, and the water was still trembling, her smoke-lens Barracuda goggles glittering on the poolside table. The pool was cool, even where the water gushed from the pump, a pucker marring the surface. I shivered. Mom stuffs all her hair into a bathing cap and swims underwater laps three or four times a week. It's a pool of ordinary backyard dimensions, but it takes lungs to pull four laps without a breath, and she can do it.

"Look out for the bug," Mom said, indicating a ladybug on its back, legs kicking. I rescued the bug, cupped her in my hand, and left the tiny red helmet floating in a small pool, wings half-cocked, ready to fly.

I waded out to the slope of the deep end. Our backyard pool is not as pristine as the one at the school, a gray patina of algae along the water-level tiles. I stretched out and floated. One of my ears was ringing, a steely, persistent drone. I freestyled shakily up and down the pool a few times, and got out of the pool and toweled off with one of Mom's old terry-cloth towels, telling myself I would not throw up.

CHAPTER

SIX

A couple of days later, Rowan came with me to watch the dive video. I was a little surprised, and pleased, because I still wasn't used to the fact that he seemed to like my company. As we walked up Lincoln Avenue toward the academy, he put one arm around me like he expected me to collapse on the sidewalk.

"What are you missing out on today?" I asked. I sounded sure of myself, but around Rowan I felt like a songbird, full of small talk. The codeine made me feel like I was walking through wet cement. Part of the problem might have been lack of sleep. Mom was always checking on me, pretending not to be worried, making sure my bedroom window was closed, offering me an extra pillow.

Rowan has a way of looking into you and seeing what's there. Gray eyes, a touch bluer than mine. He has a great hook shot, but decided he wants to concentrate on acoustical physics and meteorology. He doesn't know if he will be a sound engineer or a weatherman, but I can talk about medicine with him and he follows my line of thought. "We've been recording a saw-whet owl," he said. "There's one living in a cypress near Pescadero, off Highway One. Four nights in a row," he added. That explained the sounds of surf I had heard on the hospital phone.

He stayed right next to me, close, especially when a crack in the sidewalk made its way toward us, and when we passed a gardener buzz sawing a juniper into submission, I thought Rowan would scoop me into his arms and carry me. I dug an elbow into him and he loosened his grip. I marched ahead for a while, all the way up the hill in the June sun.

We reached the stairs down to the multi-terraced campus, and I held on to the rail. I had a dazzling three-second pain in my head.

Pain on, pain off, like a blinking red *warning*. Aside from a scraped knee now and then, I had never been injured before in my life. Dr. Breen had cautioned me to expect double vision, but on the fourth day after my accident, the day before Dad was due back from Napili Bay with his bride, I knew I had to hide the way I felt or I would be hospitalized.

I took the stairs two at a time, with a show of my usual spirit, but by the time I was heading down the open-air corridor, past the bougainvillea trellis, the world was swinging in slow, nauseating circles.

Lloyd-Fairhill is a prep school, privately endowed by rich graduates. Our school doesn't have a workaday PE department with an asphalt basketball court. It has a Jacuzzi room, and a sauna, and an arena for the swimming/diving/water polo teams with a THX sound system so you could hear your name spoken from all directions at once as you tugged your swimsuit straight. The problem with the school was that the campus was too small for all the art galleries and faculty lounges crammed into it. Softballs were always damaging the solar energy panels on the math wing, and when barn swallows built their nests over the cafeteria, you had to duck under their fluttering, swooping wings on your way to get a bowl of vegetarian chowder.

I had attended the Oakland Public Schools, but my mom had switched me to private schools partly so I could compete in water sports, and partly so I could get an education good enough to shoehorn me into a pre-med program when I got to college. It wasn't a snap decision, but Mom finally had heard enough of my descriptions of what went on in the OPS classrooms. I had an eighth-grade history teacher who taught us that the U.S. government salted the clouds over the Atlantic so all the rain would fall at sea, causing Ethiopians to die of drought. When she heard about this, Mom decided it was time to send me to an improved environment.

I would be a junior in September. After two years at Lloyd-Fairhill, I still felt awkward among kids who ate fresh-baked croissants for breakfast. My mother wrote out a check to the academy every month without a word of complaint. She was always off delivering bromeliads to model homes in Blackhawk and Pinole, and when my dad wasn't too busy sorting out his clients' lives there was a monthly check from him. We couldn't make it without the extra cash from Dad.

The doors of the academy are all painted a dazzling blue, and they are wired to a security system. Police arrested two guys over Christmas vacation for peering through the rhododendron and just thinking—merely considering—jimmying the computer lab door.

Miss P answered my knock, and I was glad to see Denise there, perched on her chair with her chin on her knees. She gave me a smile, but didn't go so far as to say good morning—she saw the look in my eyes.

"You don't want to see this," said Denise. Denise is pretty, and the dives she performs are pretty, too. She makes up for it with her mouth, always saying something no one wants to hear—something that usually happens to be true—with an accent like a gangster. Her dad arranged it so she works out with a series of personal trainers, all women, after a former tennis pro made a pass at her over Easter vacation.

"Let's get it over with," I said.

"You're sure?" asked Miss P, holding the remote like a space-age weapon you had to handle with great care. She has a way of crooking her head around from person to person, getting reassurance from everyone.

"We can put this off," said Miss P.

"Let's do it now."

"You heard her," said Denise.

34

Miss P got up and put the remote on top of the television. "Convince me," she said, and the nervous, spare person was gone.

"I can't put this off forever," I said.

"Why not?" said Miss P. She found a tube of lip balm, pulled off the cap, and applied some to her lips. "No law says if you injure yourself you have to watch the video."

"James Cagney never went to any of his own movies," said Rowan.

"That example doesn't apply," I said. Rowan's family has a massive collection of black-and-white movies in video boxes, and his dad writes articles on sound effects in films.

"It makes me sick to look at it," said Denise. Her father is a former third-string quarterback for the Oakland Raiders, and her family runs a chain of lobster and sirloin restaurants. They are warm-hearted, open people who tell each other to shut up as though this were a form of courtesy. None of them speaks in complex sentences, telling each other to pass the butter, pass the parmesan without a single *thank you.*

On the wall above the bell schedule was a glossy photo of me doing a forward flying two-and-a-half somersault off the tower. I found it a little hard to believe that this was a picture of me, that I had been that good. "Please," I said.

My friendship with Denise was often a matter of deciding which of us was stronger. She shrugged and made a show of turning away to look at a fire extinguisher.

Miss P shrank to a resigned, agreeable person. She sat beside me and pushed the fleshy buttons of the remote, and caused a jittery, streaky fast-forward to appear on the screen. A couple of the other swim team members leaped through their reverses, their half-twists, but only Denise and I practiced off the tower at the other end of the pool.

There we were, running through our reps, maybe ten dives each. Miss P stabbed the remote with her forefinger, let my image in the screen waddle jerkily to the platform, a silent-movie stuttering quality to the male figures rearranging themselves on the seats in the distance. The images slowed, settled into real time. I couldn't help appraising myself the way a diving judge does, because your dive starts the moment you toe your way out onto that cold, wet sharkskin-gritty surface of the tower.

My short blond hair pulled back, my tan, my small bust, my broad shoulders—I looked like a human being designed by God for water.

Miss P stopped it before I left the edge, rewound it. I watched again as my screen self turned halfway up the ascent to say something to someone. Smiling, but not casual. I was intent, at one point absentmindedly pulling the seat of my swimsuit. Like many swimmers and divers, I bought my swimsuits a size too tight.

At first I thought it had to be the wrong tape—even when I saw the whole dive.

Rewind, I wanted to say. At the same I wanted to close my eyes. Miss P was determined, now. If I wanted to watch she would let me, again and again. The VCR whined. I light-footed my way up the tower.

But there was nothing wrong, nothing you could see playing the tape real-time. I leaped, got good altitude on my stretch, a 9.5 beginning, and then I curled, somersaulted and it all looked okay, all the way down into the water. My entry was so-so, actually, but not terrible. If you didn't notice what Miss P did next you would expect me to haul myself dripping out of the pool to pad over to the steps and climb up all over again.

She leaped to her feet and made a front dive off poolside. She strong-armed her way to the bottom where the shifting water obliterated what was down there, the shimmering of the water defracting me into a shapeless figure Miss P pulled from the bottom, scissor kicking to the surface.

"What did I tell you," said Denise.

SEVEN

I had my nails done. I do this maybe once a year, preferring to use a pair of Revlon clippers and an emery board to keep my nails rounded and short so I won't break one off swimming laps. I sat in Lyn's Beauty Nails, soaking my pinkies in that little bowl they use, with the indentations for the fingers.

A soap opera raged in the far end of the room, where a tiny woman with carefully drawn-on eyebrows and lipstick was having a pedicure, a wife having an affair with her brother-in-law about ten inches away. "Short-short-short?" asked Lyn, sounding like she couldn't believe it.

Her name is really Nguyen, which rhymes with Lyn, more or less. She has lived in Holland and Thailand and British Columbia, one of those people you recognize as bright as soon as you see them. I told her that I was still swimming, and that I had a meet in Sacramento in a few days. Lyn nodded and went to work on my cuticle with a tiny pincers. If you haven't had your nails done professionally in a while, it's amazing all the fine,

38

membranous margin they cut away, quietly, intently, with the deft, deliberate step-by-step that reminded me too vividly of the surgeon's needle.

In drugstores the nail polish has dramatic names—Summer Tempest, Midnight Blush—but something no-nonsense about Lyn had her refer to the polish only by number, and keep a record of what she or her assistants applied in the past. "What's the matter with Ninety-one?" Lyn asked, showing me a bottle of scarlet-lady vermilion I must have picked out a year before.

When I gave myself a full-frontal look in the mirror all I saw was gray eyes, pulled-back hair, ears pierced—no earrings. Mom had asked if I had bad dreams, and I told her I couldn't remember any.

We settled on Eighty-eight—perhaps the symmetry of the number had an appeal for me. Lyn put a paper mask over her nose and mouth before she painted on the caramel-rose polish. The mask was a new development since I had visited her. Maybe the fumes were wearing out Lyn's nervous system, years of inhaling ketones giving her headaches or incipient kidney trouble. She was older than she looked, calling out in Vietnamese as children my age thumped up the stairs to the apartment above.

As she joked with the pedicure customer, expressing mock dismay at the televised crisis, Lyn stretched her arms and rotated her right wrist. The repetition was causing her some pain, using those small muscles every day, holding her arms at the same angle, pinching a nerve. I could visualize the tiny tunnels in the radius and the ulna, the paths the nerves take. I sat with my fingers in the nail dryers, twin toasters that blew hot air.

I ran through the possible scripts, what it was going to be like to meet Cindy. I know from old movies that one is supposed to say, "How do you do," fluting the words prettily, and offering a hand. But no one does that. We all say "good to meet you," or "hi." I wanted to try something new with Cindy.

I rarely fuss over what to wear and always end up sitting in the car while Mom flounces back to change earrings. I had given up on wearing jewelry, so I couldn't help feeling a kind-hearted superiority toward Mom in this regard. Now Mom was patient with me while I spread skirts and blouses all over the bed, trying to find what would match the angora beret I had bought at Nordstrom to cover the incision in my scalp.

"The trouble is, nothing really goes with this baby-blue hat," I said at last. "Why did I get angora?"

"Mmm." Meaning: Good question. But we coexist by avoiding even modestly wise-ass remarks, whenever possible, so she added, "Because it's soft and it won't itch. Here."

She stepped to the bed, selected a full-length skirt, one I wore to see *Carmen* a few months before. A white blouse, of pioneer severity, something you would see in a daguerreotype of the frontier days, a blouse I liked a lot but kept at one end of my closet. Sometimes I do this with favorite things, save them so they won't wear out or get one of those malignant tiny stains, little Bic scribbles and leaks that no chemical on earth will make vanish. She marched me into her bedroom, toe-to-toe with her full-length mirror.

Dad lives in Broadway Terrace, three blocks from where the fire stopped consuming houses and human lives several years before. I could ride my bike over, but Miss P discouraged cycling and said it stressed the wrong muscles. So I usually jogged or power-walked, which Miss P said was fine for the cardiovascular package.

When Miss P sees you at a distance she doesn't call, "Hello there," or "Good morning." She says, "Jog it," meaning: What do you think you're doing, approaching her at a mere walk? When I'm not backstroking laps I'm running up and down the stairs at the academy.

This evening, though, I didn't want to arrive all sweaty, especially in my nice clothes, which were a little tight around the waist anyway. Besides, I still had to get my final okay from Dr. Breen and had to go through another examination before I could resume my full workout schedule.

Mom drove me without having to be asked. She spent a while in her room, in a side cubicle we called "the vanity," adjusting the Shiseido natural-rose foundation she applies so artfully, and did a good job, retouching herself and brushing out her hair. She dropped me off at my dad's house early that evening, the shadows of the dwarf bamboo fluttering out across the drought-resistant landscape, buffalo grass and sage, carefully raked pea gravel.

I heard the engine of Mom's Volvo thrumming at the curb as I took the stepping stones toward the door, careful not to leave a footprint in the gravel. It was courtesy, of course, waiting to make sure my hosts were receiving me, but I could feel Mom's curiosity, too, and all the other emotions she felt sitting there with the car in neutral.

I usually opened the door with my own key, danced right in, and headed for the kitchen and a tall glass of ice water. But this time I pressed the white doorbell button and heard the baritone one-two bells, muted and solemn. And when nothing happened, I hesitated to ring them again, wondering if I had the wrong night. Because Dad is always quick to answer a telephone, hating answering machines, always jumping up in response to a knock at the door, talking all the while, hating to do only one thing at a time.

I knew it wasn't him, that light step, and when she opened the door my greetings were out before I could remember what I wanted to say. Instead I said, "Hi, I'm Bonnie," and I shook her hand like a lumberjack.

"He called to say he's running late," said Cindy. She added, gesturing to her head. "I like your tam."

A muted sound, the Volvo pulled away from the curb.

I considered whether to debate if it was a tam-o'-shanter or a beret, but instead all I said was thank you. "Running late" was a family cliché, a phrase I recognized from the dying days of my parents' marriage, but I knew something important must have kept him at the office, and that a client must have an emergency situation that needed his attention. Dad was always having to file a response to a request for summary judgment or prep an expert witness.

Still, I was disappointed, and I felt underprepared, someone called upon to give a speech to a strange audience. I followed Cindy into the kitchen when she asked me, would I like anything. She must have expected me to sit in the living room, admiring the coffee-table books I had never seen before, *Chinese Jade for the Collector, Cloissonné Masterpieces*. I followed her right in and accepted a glass of pineapple juice with three big cubes of ice.

"I really like this house," she said. A car approached in the street, and we both paused to listen. The distant engine murmur traveled on up the neighborhood.

Maybe she was telling me that she hadn't really overnighted here very often. Maybe she was complimenting me, assuming that I had helped my dad pick out the English fox-hunter prints and the books on the glories of the quarter horse. For someone just back from Hawaii, she didn't have much of a tan.

She had been Dad's secretary for about a year and a half, but when I called my dad I almost always spoke to one of the receptionists, a series of temps. I had only visited my Dad's new office a couple of times, and admired its view of Lake Merritt and the other neighboring office buildings. Ever since my dad and his law partner, Adam David, had split up a couple of years ago, my dad's schedule had been too frenzied for anyone but him to keep track of. So far, he was only ten minutes late.

"I'm not going to do anything to the landscaping," Cindy was saying, perhaps on the theory that if my mom liked root systems and broad-leafs, then it was only natural that I did, too. I felt a little sorry for her suddenly. She was a woman just a little older than my sister Georgia, stuck with a stepdaughter who kept giving her a thousand-yard stare.

"I always thought Dad overdid it with bamboo," I said.

She kept peeling the Saran wrap off the rosemary chicken, nudging it with a fork to make sure it was still there.

Sometimes Cindy would glance up, a morsel of chicken breast poised on her fork, mistaking yet another passing car for Dad's BMW. But unless the car sounded a lot like Dad's I was rarely deceived. As the evening went on and Dad called again, we settled into stories of Cindy's childhood. She had grown up in Nevada, Iowa—pronounced with a long *a*: Ne-*vay*-da. "They make everything out of soy, ink and food, so my dad raised that, but what he loved was livestock."

When I told Cindy her books about collectibles were an improvement over Dad's usual reading matter, the Kentucky Derby and bare-fisted boxing, Cindy said that she was going to invest in transportable assets. This was the one phrase she used that made me stop and look sideways at her as I sipped my pineapple juice, wondering if this was the sort of thing you said if you were raised around abandoned silos. Her fingernails were the same color as mine, but longer.

Dad called yet again, and Cindy said things were great, do what you have to do. I could feel the conversation filling with things she didn't want to mention, even when she took the portable phone into the den, where Dad kept the largely un-read, leather-bound volumes he had inherited from his grand-father, Emerson and Dickens and geographies of a world that doesn't exist anymore.

Finally, at the end of the third call, Cindy waved me into the den and I stood staring at the spine of Byron's collected poems while Dad said he was sorry he had made such a mess of the evening, he would make it up to me. He was helping Mrs. Jovanovich.

Cindy drove me home after we had picked at our pine-nut tarts, fresh baked that day at Angelino's in Montclair. As she dropped me off at my mom's house, Cindy thanked me for coming over, as if I had done her a big personal favor. I couldn't bring myself to say you're welcome, staring into the silhouette of her head, her hair the kind that doesn't take much of a curl, a lank wave down to each shoulder. I told her I wanted to hear more about tornadoes.

Mrs. Jovanovich was a white-haired woman who walked with two silvery canes. Her family had owned land near Pebble Beach, and her husband had been a television producer. Now her only daughter lived in England, and Dad shepherded her estate through insurance payments, lease agreements, even helping her buy a new hearing aid when an improved model was advertised. This was typical of the kind of support Dad gave his clients, and it was clear to me that Mrs. Jovanovich must have suffered some heart flutter or the legal equivalent of a fainting spell that kept him on the phone to London or to a doctor.

But when Mom asked how did it go, looking up from a mess of paperwork, I didn't know what to tell her. She meant: Tell me you father didn't marry a cliché blonde, a brainless flirt. But I didn't want to go into detail and have to tell her that Dad had never shown up.

"She knows all about hogs," I said.

"No kidding," said Mom, with greater interest than I expected.

"You don't want to live downwind," I said. "If you raise too many pigs per acre it's bad for the water table. The manure soaks into the ground."

"Harvey must love hearing about that every night," she said. Everyone called my Dad by his entire first name, never Harv.

"Hogs ate a boy's fingers off," I said, since the subject seemed to intrigue Mom. "He passed out from the fumes, and the animals thought he was fodder," using Cindy's exact words.

The drive from Oakland to Sacramento takes a couple of hours, some one hundred miles through metropolitan fringe, dairy-cow hills, and at last the flat pasture land that used to be an inland sea, according to Rowan. In prehistoric time, he means, although sometimes during winter a levee breaks and again the valley turns into ocean.

Denise suffers from hay fever, and she is almost superstitious about taking antihistamines before a meet, worried they might make her pee test come out false-positive. I tell her this is unlikely in the extreme, but athletes trust suffering.

Some schools rent little yellow school busses, or own cute little vans with REDWOOD PREPARATORY or CARMEL HIGH SCHOOL lettered on the door panel. The academy rents air-conditioned Peerless Stage busses, the same conveyances gamblers charter for the long trip to Reno. The bus was not half full, even with the chaperones, the volunteer supervisors, wives of dentists, and professors on sabbatical. The seats have head cushions, and the armrests have obsolete ashtrays, little metal doors you can flip open and see the old freckles of ash even professional maintenance cannot completely remove. The seats cushions are green velour, very comfy.

Denise and I are among the leading lights of the swim and dive team, and we are also the youngest members, so the other athletes leave us alone. There is no chill involved, it's all amiable. But Denise and I often lunch together, or swing into the back seat of a bus, and they give us a nod or a wave and let us be. Miss P came to the rear of the bus, hand to hand along the seat backs, asking if Denise was okay.

"Snot," said Denise, sounding like someone talking from inside a pillow. "My head is full of it."

Miss P shook her head sympathetically and hunched to get a better view of the dry, empty fields. "Adrenaline will clear it," said Miss P, and this was true. A sudden shock, or anticipating the gaze of five thousand strangers, will clear your sinuses before you even suit up.

"My head feels like it's this big," said Denise almost peacefully.

"I'm allergic to acacia," said Miss P, and I could see that the coach needed to keep her mind occupied, too.

I wasn't scheduled to dive. I had put on a show of disappointment, looking around at things with a hard, frustrated glare, but as I sat there watching the dried-up scenery go by, I was relieved.

I didn't know how I would feel, watching my friends compete. Maybe I wouldn't be able to look without my ears ringing, the pain coming back.

Miss P had been legendary as a coach who made her athletes run fifteen laps if someone giggled during roll call. But by the time I got to the academy Miss P had lost weight, dwindling from the hardy, tanned brunette who took the top members of the academy swim team to three bronzes in the Goodwill Games a few years ago.

She was still a good coach—a better coach now, in a way, because a touch of frailty made her athletes patient with her if she forgot her whistle or had to sit down during touch-and-go, the relay laps we swim by the hour. She had stayed with me while we watched the videotaped accident backward and forward, until I could see what happened with my eyes closed, my head kissing the edge of the platform.

Sacramento is a sprawling, flat town, with trees blue in the distance, mirage shivering the streets. One step out of the bus and

I wanted to climb right back in. Denise made an exaggerated stagger, like someone who's been shot, but it was no joke. The weather report had said it would hit one hundred and five Fahrenheit, and it felt way hotter than that all the way across the asphalt parking lot.

Parking attendants with EVENT STAFF on their backs in yellow letters squinted around at things, talking into handheld radios, probably to make sure their colleagues had not succumbed to heat stroke. The academy men trailed off with a male assistant, Mr. Browning, the guy who shot the videos, and the women angled into our own facility, but you could see when we split up how few we were.

Our team had a corner of the locker room, a roomy place used by professional teams hardly anyone in Oakland knows anything about, a football league with teams in cities like Salt Lake City and Barcelona, and soccer teams who play in front of nine loyal fans. But marginal pro teams still have plush facilities, and we enjoyed the feel of carpeting under our toes, and lockers big enough to accommodate half a wardrobe.

Swimmers tried on their goggles, took them off, untangled the straps, tugged them on again. Denise climbed into her black swimsuit and put on the red-and-white warm-up togs Miss P insists on, telling us we have to wear our colors whenever we represent the academy.

I wore exactly what Denise was wearing, and what they all wore. I kept my eyes up, looking people in the eye, zipped all the way to my chin even in the Martian-surface heat we had to single-file our way through. I didn't want to look in the direction of the platform. I wondered if it was a mistake to be there at all.

I forced myself to watch the swimmers in their preliminary heats, my ears ringing. I sat on the bench while Denise did her dive, screwing up every time, especially on her entry. A front dive is a plain dive, but if your entry is good—the rip you make entering the water—the judges love it. If it looks like nothing has happened, it goes well. One minute the diver is erect on the tower, and the next she's gone, hardly a ripple.

In Denise's case there was a ripple. On all three dives. A splash, water all over the place. And each time you could see what a mistake it was. You could see it in Denise's eyes each time she came out of the pool. Miss P looked at me and shook her head in apology to me, to the team. But I stood up and clapped my hands, and each time I told Denise how well she had done.

CHAPTER

NINE

Swimming arenas are a wash of noise, reverberating whistles, shouted encouragement. Some divers wear earplugs to escape the surreal murmur of the crowd. Even a huge place fills with the smell of the lifeless water.

I kept busy on the bench, handing out the blue Speedo WaterShed towels we use instead of terry cloth, but I hated meeting Miss P's eyes. The wound in my scalp tingled, itched. The WaterShed towels are rubbery and specially treated—one wipe and you're dry. We still use regular cloth towels as a hood—to sit under if you don't want people to see your face.

Charlotte Witt, an academy senior with seasons of competitive experience, led the field after the preliminary round, doing a front dive layout with a difficulty rating of only 1.2, a springboard dive. Charlotte was a very good diver, but this late in her high school career she was developing too much of a figure and too much of a concentration problem.

"You don't have to do this," Miss P said, leaning close to me. "You can go in and take a rest."

I waved her away.

"You look rotten," said Denise. I felt like telling her that if I had done so badly on my difficulty-zero dives I would keep my mouth shut. Denise and I liked to run or swim laps together, and she laughed at the same books I do, where the author proves space aliens built the Great Pyramids and invented Oreos. Sometimes I wished she had chronic laryngitis.

I had to go into the locker room and lie down on a bench. Even in there I could hear the endless babble, a cavern of faceless voices beyond the metal doors.

Dad had called just before I left to catch the bus, and I didn't have the heart to tell him that I hadn't gotten medical clearance. I had never even mentioned my injury. I conned myself into half believing I didn't want to cause him any worry. I knew he was proud of me for earning a write-up in the *Chronicle*, "Prep Platform Promise," although they had not run the picture the paper had spent an hour getting from various angles, me in midair. Dad wished me luck, and then, putting on his confidential voice, he said, "You were real good with Cindy."

I had been sitting on my bed, one shoe off, one shoe on, glad to hear his voice at last, and yet I couldn't help bridling a little at his phrasing. "Of course I was *good*," I said, serving the word back to him.

"We'll take the boat out this weekend," he said.

Cindy had told me, in complete seriousness, that it was all right to have a painted still life with fruit on a plate in the dining room. She had read it in a magazine. I listened for some sign in Dad's voice of what he might see in Cindy, wondering at the power sex has over people. And Cindy wasn't even terribly pretty—she was all right, in a tepid, Bo-Peep way but didn't have the kind of looks Mom has when she really tries.

"We'll go out and see if any whales are migrating," he was saying.

Dad has no idea when whales migrate, what they eat, or whether or not they poop in the water. But I was grateful for the effort he was making. "I bet the boat has barnacles all over it," I said, so pleased at the idea of going out on the bay that I couldn't express it.

A company called Marine Core power-vacuumed *Queen Athena*'s hull, and Dad himself called me from the motor yacht sometimes, using the boat as a weekend office. I don't think he took it out more than three times a year, but it was his pride. His only hobby was caring for the *Queen*, rubbing tung oil on the teak finishing, experimenting with brass polish and chemicals that killed mildew.

Lying on a locker room bench is not reassuring. The benches are slatted wood and narrow, and it is easy to have the illusion that you are ten thousand feet up on a plank, one move and you plummet. I kept telling one of the dentist-wife moms that I was all right, every time she bustled in to check.

I had to pull the earphones off my head. I was listening to one of Miss P's favorites, a tape on concentrating your mind. Waves crash, and wind blows through grasses, and it sounds a lot like the recordings Rowan and his parents make, except that a man's voice tells you to imagine things. I would hear a discordant female voice saying my name, and I would have to stir myself from My Own Private Landscape and tell a woman who probably couldn't even swim that I was down-stressing.

"You sure?" she would say each time, lipstick and frosted hair.

I wasn't light-headed, and I wasn't seeing double. I wanted to turn the volume all the way up, high enough to damage my ears, so I wouldn't have to hear the endless, lapping sounds of the dives. And my own nagging inner voice: If I couldn't even stand to watch, what was going to happen when Dr. Breen said I was cleared to dive?

After the day's competition, we ate at a Chinese restaurant near the state capitol, Denise and I sharing a baked fish that arrived looking like a dragon, mouth agape, roasted eyeballs staring. Denise asked the waiter to take off the head so she wouldn't have to look at it. Her dad calls her "Princess," and had Bausch & Lomb custom design prescription goggles so she could have 20/20 vision underwater.

Miss P said it was okay to open the fortune cookies, and if the fortune was bad it would come true only if we ate some of the cookie. She laughed, but she looked tired, more weary than a coach should, with one day of elimination over and plenty of scoring to come.

I hunted around among the cracked-open cookies. The fortunes were on little paper tabs that scatter and soak up spilled tea. There were two kinds of fortunes: *You are outgoing and have many friends*, the blazing compliment. *You will make a fortune and travel widely*, the golden lie.

If I worked in a cookie factory I would write fortunes that would help improve the world. *Three incredibly delightful things will happen to you if you recycle aluminum for a year.* I opened a new cookie, read the little white slip, and handed it to Miss P across the table. It told her she won respect wherever she went.

She read it and smiled thank you.

"You were okay," I told Denise that night, kicking my feet to loosen the strait-jacket covers. *Okay* can mean a lot of different things. *The hamburgers are okay* can mean: Take these away, no one can eat them.

"I was shit," she said. She was watching television, aiming the remote but not using it.

We were in the Holiday Inn, right beside the Interstate 80 Alternate. You could walk under the freeway and visit Old Town, shops where they sold raspberry ropes and licorice chews, and the shop clerks wore derby hats. Tourists licked pistachio nut and pumpkin sherbet ice cream cones, but we were forbidden what Miss P called *glop,* so after a quick peek at the postcard racks we had scurried back to the inn, safe and snug by curfew.

"It just wasn't your best day," I conceded gently.

Denise snapped off the television and gave me a steady look. The whites of her eyes were bloodshot. The goggles make her look like a frog; she leaves them at home. She thinks the bathing cap she wears makes her look like a classic diver from the fifties. "Be honest with me, Bonnie," she said.

My voice is all springtime and daisies compared with Denise's gangster contralto. I didn't really want to be frank with her—she wasn't as calm as she looked. "Okay."

"I've never had a worse day, right?"

Sometimes you just don't want to cause that little extra bit of pain.

"I was that bad," she said. *So bad you can't even express it.*

But Denise's dives hadn't been shockingly terrible—just a matter of awkward timing. And no poise—she had lost her calm, bunching her jaw, diving like someone smashing through a cinderblock wall. "I've seen a lot worse," I said.

"You're telling me everything I need to know," she said.

"I didn't say a single negative."

"Thank you, Bonnie," she said, running her fingers through her dark hair.

"I didn't *say* anything!"

I wished Miss P had gotten the kind of fortune she deserved: *Good news will arrive from an unexpected quarter.*

CHAPTER

TEN

By the time I reached berth 101 I could see that the day wasn't going to go the way I had pictured it.

Cindy was leaning against the taffrail, looking at the boats and bare masts all around us through binoculars. Perhaps I had expected a quiet, father/daughter day in the sun, Cindy demurely in the background. I must have been a huge, weird image through the Leitz binoculars, legging my way down the gangway, because she gave a little start and said, "Golly!"

But it was the presence of Jack Stoughton that made me take a moment before I stepped down into the *Queen,* not wanting to see Jack or have him see me. Not that we ever say any more than hi to each other. Jack Stoughton defends people Denise knows, money launderers and basketball players three years behind in their child support payments. He's good at it, always driving a new Jaguar or a bright red two-seater of a make no one else ever heard of. Jack had gone to school with Dad—they played tennis together on the asphalt courts in Strawberry Canyon.

Dad looked out from the cabin door just to one side of the

helm, and he gave me one of his waves, one hand up, like someone far away. He looked wonderful, tanned, a little white mark on his nose from wearing sunglasses. He was motioning Jack into the cabin, where a miniature galley and a miniature bathroom and a bedroom/living room were nestled into the hull, neat and homey.

"Bonnie," Jack boomed, not dressed for boating, which gave me a little hope. He wore a rust-brown suit, matching his red hair and his red eyebrows. He cocked his head and gave me a smile he should have practiced in front of a mirror, showing where some bridgework on the left side of his upper jaw was missing. Then Jack, too, vanished into the cabin, reaching back to pull the door shut.

"Jack's on the clock," said Cindy, looking around at pointless things with the binoculars Dad kept stowed along with the bird book and the spare batteries. She meant: Dad would be billed for this visit, down to the minute. One of Dad's habitual gestures is a glance at his sport watch, which he wears with the watch face on the pulse of his wrist. I've watched him making notes in a red leather book when he gets done with one phone call and starts another, getting up to shut the den door, protecting client privilege.

"Dad's throwing him some business," I said, not really interested, just accepting the fact that it would be a while.

Cindy shrugged, but she kept peering at distant cars and people swabbing decks or flaking out rope in tidy Flemish loops.

"You wouldn't want to have a boat like that," she said, indicating a dazzling white sailing yacht purling out toward the bay under temporary mechanical power, its crew of four leaning against the port rail, flexing their shoulders, getting ready for some white-canvas sailing.

I wanted to respond that I sure would, but Cindy looked worn today, little wrinkles under her eyes, and I pawed through my carryall for some sunblock.

She applied the stuff with two fingers, squinting and gaping like someone smearing on night cream. "It would be hard to park a big yacht like that," she was saying.

I agreed that it might take practice.

"What happened here?" she said, pointing above her own ear.

I didn't say anything. I touched the bare place on my head, the fine little stitches. Fuzz was already filling in the naked skin.

"Better put some goop on it," she said.

I appreciated her good sense, but didn't want the coconut oil in my hair. Still, I accepted her attentions, her gentle dab, dab, and when the two men emerged you could see Jack approving, women involved in petty activities, grooming each other.

But this wasn't the way I wanted to introduce the subject of my injury, so I flung the scarf over my head for a moment, peasant fashion.

"Later," Dad called to Jack, and big as our boat is, she lifted and fell when Jack disembarked and hurried up the gangway, folding papers into an interior pocket of his jacket.

"Champion!" said Dad, and he gave me a hug. I was a little

embarrassed. Champion is one of his pet names for me, and here was Cindy looking on. But he was also letting me know that his feelings for me were the same as ever, and he was letting Cindy in on this, too. He didn't comment on the blue-and-white scarf knotted under my chin.

As we rumbled past the Alameda Coast Guard station, Cindy wanted to know why the navy painted its ships red and white. I told her they were rescue cutters, and you'd be glad to see them if you were clinging to a floating mast off the Farrallons. Maybe I misrepresented my grasp of sea lore a little, explaining to her that there were two kinds of cutters, one a variety of sailboat, not at all like one of these powerful small ships. I can read a compass, and a depth chart is no mystery, but I have trouble calling a toilet "the head."

"I took swimming lessons," she asserted.

"You didn't!" said Dad, steady at the helm, not looking at either of us.

"The Australian crawl," said Cindy. She headed back across the boat, and focused the binoculars on another sight too close to be worth looking at through eight by twenty-four glasses, a gray ship taking on a stream of shiny metal, scrap entering her cargo hold with a grinding roar like a garbage disposal. Even with the light wind drifting from the west you could smell the processed metal, a sour stink.

"Australian crawl," said Dad, with a wink at me. No one calls it that anymore. "Bonnie'll rescue you."

"In Ames," she said. "Fulfilling the PE requirement. I was the best in the class."

She said this in a pertly serious way, and Dad was quick to say that he had no doubt she was the best in every category.

"My Great-Uncle Carl was nearly killed by a torpedo," she said.

"What did you do with that pill?" Dad asked his bride as we powered north toward the Bay Bridge, the water calm, the air beginning to freshen. This was the way an experienced lawyer asks questions—not Did you swallow the medicine? or Did you lose the tablet?—never leading the witness.

"I took it," said Cindy sounding resigned, or embarrassed.

"You're going to need it," said Dad.

By the time the shadow of the Golden Gate Bridge fell over us Cindy was leaning back on a cushion in the cabin, swearing that the seasickness pill would kick in any minute.

I got her a plastic pan from the galley, the kind a boat carries for really no other purpose. I sat with her. "He was on a troop ship going to Europe, and they had the wolf packs," she said. "The submarines?" She said this with a questioning tone, as though offering an answer she thought might be wrong.

I couldn't follow her thread of conversation for a moment. I must have murmured something, because she added, "He heard the torpedo hit with a clang. But it didn't go off."

When I got a wet hand towel from the bathroom—the head—she said that I was wasting my time, she would die soon. She said it as a joke, but her lips were gray.

CHAPTER

ELEVEN

I had to grab a rail and hang on. The wind was stiffening, the radio antenna lashing back and forth. I couldn't help feeling a stab of compassion for Cindy, below deck, half out of her bunk.

Dad shook his head happily and shouted something about not being able to get the maximum out of the *Queen* today. Or maybe he was yelling merrily that he was going to plunge us all deep into the Pacific. Dad had always driven the forty-eight-foot Super Sport toward its limit, thirty knots when a swell wasn't running. The boat tore through the moderate seas, and a large ship, a coursing building, loomed down on us.

I was aware of how much I had been looking forward to conversation, chitchat, how snorkeling had been. I had been wondering if Dad might want a kitten in a couple of months—maybe two kittens. He often took in strays, although he had terrible luck with them, always having to drive them to the vet. Myrna's kittens still looked like dirty socks, but they were at the crawling stage, their eyes beginning to open.

I suspected it was against some law to slash through the water in shirtsleeves, none of the passengers equipped with life vests. The tanker made a subtle adjustment, the faceless bulk steering by telepathy, and when the giant vessel was past us, Dad swung the helm to slice across the wake.

The container ship loomed, so breathtakingly close I felt the cool damp of its shadow, but this was pure Dad, grinning as our bow wave plastered the windshield with salt water and drenched my silk scarf so it hung on me chilly and wet. Dad had ordered the *Queen* custom crafted from a boatbuilder in Egg Harbor, New Jersey, and in the four years since he had first eased her out of the berth he had always looked forward to pounding his way through choppy water, forgetting all about fuel efficiency.

"How's your tennis?" he shouted over the thrum of the engine, and it sounded like he was calling, *How's your dentist?*

Dad eased off on the throttle, gulls capering along the lacy trough in the water. Some of the gulls were gray, drab, a year or two old, and some were older, elegant and pristine in their adult uniforms. I said something about not having much time to practice.

"I'm going to give Cindy lessons," he said. "We'll make a threesome."

In his den Dad had a shelf of nothing but Wimbledon on videotape. "The two of us against your forehand smash," I said, playing along, just to keep him in such a good mood.

"Why not?" There were little flecks of water on his sunglasses. They would dry there, leaving brine spots, so I stooped into the galley for some paper towels. Cindy was a huddled thing, boneless, beyond the bulkhead. I gave the towel a squirt of Windex and wiped his glasses for him. I was stalling, giving myself some time to remember the last time I had picked up a tennis racket, Rowan and I not even bothering to keep score.

"Tell me why not?" he persisted, allowing me to hook the aviator glasses over his ears.

I lifted one shoulder, let it fall, happy but unwilling to commit. My family takes sports like a religion. I was scheduled to see Dr. Breen on Friday before lunch.

"You're chicken," he said offhandedly.

Dad used a set of old-fashioned epithets when he teased or when he stubbed his toe on one of his own briefcases. You were "chicken" if you insisted on donning a life vest, or "a heel" if you didn't send someone a get-well card, or "a piker" if you bought the cheapest meal on the menu. I don't know where he got these words, and no one else I have ever met used quite this vocabulary. When he stubbed his toe he said "*Judas Priest*," the closest he ever came to swearing.

But there was a trace of challenge to the sidelong glance he gave me. Dad *owns* tennis, possesses it entirely—he might have invented the sport personally, down to the sweet spot in the rackets and the fuzz on the balls. He has two serves. Serve One is a gunshot, blinding fast. If that attack is long or wide, Serve Two is a lob, gentle and spooky, with a magical backspin. Every time I'd seen him play Jack Stoughton, the big red-haired man ended up reaching for his wallet, another bet lost.

"Friday night," he called, gunning the engine. Then he hit the side of his head, an exaggerated "I almost forgot."

He slipped a velvet box from his pants pocket.

The box alone was luxurious, my fingers leaving silvery prints on the lavender plush.

He gave me an *open it* lift of his chin.

"They dive three hundred feet down for those pearls," he said. "Holding their breath."

"No they don't." I laughed.

"*You* could."

We headed toward the Golden Gate, back in toward the harbor. The shadow of the bridge was cool as we surged through it, and the wind from behind whipped the knot ends of my scarf up around my lips.

Mom didn't ask, not in so many words. She did inquire how everything was, that inclusive Everything that means the weather, human life, my father. She didn't take the pearl out of its box. She said it was nice.

But it was only when we were in her shop very early Friday morning that she said, "They won't have kids, will they." A statement, a definite assertion, as she fastened her green smock, bending to her most recent shipment.

I could have said, *How would I know.* But the question was hard-edged, a consideration I had avoided. The last years of my parents' difficulties had taken place behind the closed door of their bedroom, but I had overheard my dad's whiplash whisper

HEAT

and his upbeat laugh: There, I've made a point. Mom can deal with tax accountants, and she can fire a cashier if the till is fifteen cents short, but in an argument she gets a stubborn, feline expression and just waits for the disagreement to pass.

Tropical plants often arrive wrapped in bright-colored plastic, customs stickers and aphis-control tabs stuck on randomly. Mom stops talking when she unwraps a special order, using a tiny knife blade and a quiet, peering manner as she works, as though if the plant inside is blighted she can catch just a glimpse and stop right there, and not have to expose herself to full disappointment.

"This is supposed to be a white bird-of-paradise," she said, palpating the plastic wrapper, scarlet OVERNIGHT and RUSH taped over the seams. A photographer for the Sunday *Examiner* was shooting a spread at Dunsmuir house, a historical mansion on the bank of Lake Merritt.

I stood by with a pair of iron shears, like someone ready to kill the specimen if it proved monstrous. If a bird-of-paradise is anything less than perfectly healthy it turns into black slime. I said something encouraging, and Mom continued to worry the shipping tape, unpeeling plastic.

When the shipment was completely undressed, Mom peered at it through her half-lens glasses, examining each blue spike. I didn't want to be late to see Dr. Breen, but I knew how fussy photographers can be. They insist that even the most rare exotics show up garden fresh—the hot lights kill blossoms in a few hours.

CHAPTER

TWELVE

Dr. Breen's office was completely bare. Little steel hooks glittered on the walls where paintings had been removed, and aside from the examination table, with its required length of white butcher paper, and a small side desk, the doctor's office was empty, the workplace of a person getting ready to flee the country. "Doctor will be right in," said a nurse, one of those human dumplings who really should read up on cholesterol.

I was never going to put a patient through anything like this.

Dr. Breen herself was wearing something knit and slinky, a dress with a drop waist, mauve and very unusual, from what I could see of it through her unbuttoned lab coat. She gave me one bright look, up and down, taking me in the way men sometimes do, and then went back to the folders in her hands, leaning on her desk. She straightened her back, continuing to read.

"I'm sorry to be so late," she said at last.

I heard myself say that I didn't mind. Maybe one tiny part of my mind hadn't wanted Dr. Breen to show up, and didn't want to ever climb the tower again. I asked what color she was going to paint the walls.

"Whatever color the architecture committee picks," she said, looking through my folder. "What do you think—nerve white? Bone marrow pink?"

I gave a little pro forma laugh.

She pried a paper clip free, nodding as she read. "How have you been feeling?" not looking up.

"Great."

This got her attention. "You haven't experienced—"

"Double vision, no."

I answered no to nausea, dizziness, and told her promptly that my appetite was fine.

"And the event-specific amnesia."

"I've been remembering it in sections." I had prepared this statement, having anticipated the question, and it came out a little wooden.

"Have you?" Friendly, but not friendly.

I had to offer her something, something true. I had to give her some hint how I felt. "I have dreams."

Her gaze slipped off mine for an instant, as though dreams were not her field of expertise. "What of?"

"The dive," I said. I couldn't keep from sounding a little exasperated—why else would I mention this? "The accident."

She gave me the little wrinkle of a smile I had noticed before, as though "accident" were a euphemism.

"I didn't get the right altitude," I said. "And then, because of

69

that, I didn't have the leverage when I tucked in. Of course, I could have hit my toes. A guy in San Diego broke a metatarsal a few months ago, dinging the tower with his foot. I could have missed and gotten away with it. But I didn't."

"You can't remember it."

"It doesn't matter."

"It's all right that you can't recall the actual dive, step by step."

"That's what I mean—I know it's all right."

"Tell me about the dream," she said.

"What made you choose neurology?" I asked. One way to cross-examine an expert witness successfully is to mix up your questions, keep the witness just a little off guard.

She looked at me with her polite smile. Her makeup was good.

"You could have picked—radiology," I said, imagining her scurrying into the control booth, protecting her reproductive future from the electromagnetic waves.

"Radiologists are the most boring people in the world," she said, slipping out of her doctor voice for a second, as though visualizing radiologists at parties, next to her in meetings, excited about their new high-speed Kodak film.

I wanted to be an ophthalmologist. I wanted to cure blindness, and I wasn't afraid to imagine my touch searching the vitreous humor, the central fluid of the eyeball, for a steel splinter or a shard of glass.

I had sometimes given into fantasies of my waiting room, with broad, comfortable chairs, easy for the sight impaired to find, with simple, beautiful abstract paintings, greens and blues, on the walls. I had fantasies I was a little embarrassed by, tall, soft-voiced male nurses telling frightened but increasingly hopeful patients, "Dr. Chamberlain will see you now." But I had studied the university catalogs carefully, Duke, Harvard, Stanford. Dad had always said cost was no object.

I told Dr. Breen about my dreams, putting some feeling into it.

"These nightmares trouble you," she suggested, gently.

I hesitated. "A little."

"I never remember my dreams. I'm going through a divorce, and I would like to have access to whatever my unconscious might have to offer in the way of dream commentary. But—"

This happens to me—people look at me, make a judgment about my character, and tell me about themselves. "That's too bad," I said. "About not dreaming."

"I've always envied people who had howling nightmares. Wonderful story dreams. Rich inner lives."

"You're right to envy us. It's wonderful."

She laughed, looking a little like my sister Georgia.

"I'm signing a release," she said, briskly hurrying back to her doctor diction. "This form—"

She said *form* with a trace of exasperation, another scrap of paperwork to clutter her life. She let a piece of stationery flutter in her hand, extended in my direction, *Lloyd-Fairhill Academy* in dignified Medieval-looking script at the top.

"I'm clearing you," she said.

CHAPTER

THIRTEEN

The ten-meter platform has no bounce to it, not like a diving board. The diver doesn't experience any of that buoyant, walking-the-plank give under her feet. It's like standing on the outthrust edge of a building.

All the energy for her leap must come from her own body, from her legs, from the sudden fulcrum of her own length, stretched high. She folds her arms around her knees, creating an axis. To spin faster she goes into a tighter tuck, becomes a smaller circle.

Sometimes you begin your climb up the steps in chilly winter shadow and reach the apex of the dive in the heat of a summer afternoon. In the vacation resorts my parents enjoyed, even in the sunset days of their marriage, I always worked on my dives. In pools in Palm Springs and Vegas, I did layouts and pikes off the glittering white sandpaper of the springboards. I practiced half twists and curls, wishing I could go higher, wishing I could soar.

"She was born to it" was the way Mom put it. Even during the trial separation, Dad paid the monthly membership at the Skyline Country Club, until the instructor there said she had nothing more to teach me.

A woman from the *Tribune* asked me once if I was ever afraid, and I said, "Of what?"

I didn't say anything to Mom in the waiting room, I just put the release form right down in front of her, on top of the article about the birds of the tundra.

All the way home Mom drove faster than usual, shaking her head and making a little laugh through her nose. She kept looking at the release form at every stoplight.

I smoothed the form out on my knee, although it wasn't wrinkled, taking care with it. *J. T. Breen.*

My hands were cold.

You don't wear pretty shorts and bright colored, classic tennis tops to battle my father. I dressed like someone getting ready to help Mom dig up a tree stump, cuffed khaki shorts and an over-size blue T-shirt. My racket is carbon and steel, a gift from Dad a couple of Christmases ago, a better racket than my tennis game deserved. Mom asked, "Why the long face?"

"I'm not ready for this" was all I said, making myself sound ironic and lighthearted. I zipped the racket into its carrier, yet another gift from Dad, a three-hundred-dollar gym bag with a side pocket for tennis gear. Mom, who once had burst into tears in a match against Dad at the Hotel Coronado, put her hands on her hips, waiting for me to talk.

I gave her a sigh exactly like one of her own, an utterly false, it's-just-a-game, which should not have deceived her for a second. The clearance form was on the dining room table.

I took my time on the long walk to Dad's, hating myself for not practicing my serve with a phantom ball, just to work off some of the rust. I knew Cindy was one of those false novices, someone who insists they haven't held a racket since they were eleven years old and then backhands every living creature into submission.

At least all of this distracted me from my feelings, my sensation of dread.

As I approached Dad's neighborhood of men waxing sports cars, watering their drought-flouting lawns in the long, early evening glow, I began to jog and felt a little more loose, a little more centered. Miss P tells us to visualize the dive going right, to imagine it that way every time, and to see ourselves into the water.

I pictured myself stopping one of Dad's lobs at the net, chopping it, getting spin on the ball. I imagined myself legging my way left and right, Cindy looking on, as I handled Dad myself. "You've been practicing!" Dad would say, surprised, mistaken.

The front door was open, so even as I pressed the doorbell, the high-low bronze notes sounding somewhere within the walls,

HEAT

I was already on my way inside. I called for Dad, and for Cindy, force of habit sending me toward the kitchen for a glass of water.

They were in the dining room, the two of them, Jack Stoughton and Cindy. My first impression was that I had interrupted an intimate moment between them. They were having an affair, and I was too astonished to feel the outrage that was already on its way in some part of my mind.

But then I saw the crumpled Kleenex in Cindy's hand, a white tissue so wadded and worn it was nearly reduced to lint. Jack wore one of his auburn-brown suits, but his hair was hastily combed, red strands starting away from his head. He looked directly at me and did not speak.

"Oh, Bonnie," said Cindy, in the tone she would have used to get my attention as I was about to leave. I knew what she was about to say—that she had forgotten about me, about our tennis date.

"What's wrong?" I asked.

Cindy said nothing.

My mouth was dry. I asked, "Where's Dad?"

Jack was taller than I remembered, and his eyebrows were white.

"Your father," he said, in a very gentle voice, "has been arrested."

FOURTEEN

Arrested, I thought.

As in *The spread of the disease has been arrested.* It was almost possible to twist the words I had heard into good news—except for the way Cindy was destroying the tissue in her hands.

Jack pursed his lips, preliminary to speech. He was going to pick his words with care, charging by the minute.

Then I realized that Dad must have backed the *Queen* into a sailboat in a neighboring berth, or perhaps he had fallen into one of those webby, legal hazards, an unpaid parking ticket showing up on the computer when a cop gives you a ticket for a broken taillight. But Cindy was braced in the chair, looking across the walnut reflection of the dining table as if it and the rest of the room were all about to vanish. Jack approached me, lifted a hand, and almost let it fall on my shoulder.

"We'll get it all put right," said Jack.

I recognized the oddly British phrasing of the legal world, a verbal landscape that has chain-smoking divorce specialists inserting *Esquire* after their names.

The expression on my face made him change his vocabulary, and even his voice sounded more regular-guy. "This kind of thing happens," said Jack, standing close to me, but not touching.

"What kind of thing?" I asked, a little surprised that I could make a sound.

Jack turned to Cindy, as if to let her know that he would say nothing, or tell all, it was up to her.

"It's a misunderstanding, " said Jack. He tilted his head to one side, *I can't talk right now.*

"They won't post bail until Monday," said Cindy, in an oddly steady voice, despite the trembling fingers she ran through her hair. It was easy to imagine that she had been good at her job, shepherding a law practice.

"He's in jail for the weekend," I said, partly to let them know that they could talk to me, I knew my way around. And also as a reality check—I wanted them to say no, of course that's not what we mean.

"The district attorney planned it this way," said Cindy in her small, no nonsense voice. "They waited until Friday afternoon to execute the warrant, and he has to spend the weekend in custody. In Santa Rita," she added. "There's an injunction against admitting any more inmates to the jail in Oakland because of overpopulation." She rubbed a hand up and down her forearm as she said this.

I found myself at her side, my hand on her shoulder, the way Jack had almost comforted me. She looked up at me, her eyes blank but steady. Santa Rita jail was far east of Oakland, in a dry valley near a golf course. Cattle grazed and barns gradually decomposed in the heat. I had passed it a few times on the bus, going to swim and dive meets in Modesto and Bakersfield. It appeared to be a very large, somber junior high school, with guard towers.

Jack rested his hand on the back of a chair. "Your father's always had his critics," he said.

Crooked building contractors, I thought. Insurance companies who didn't cough up after a fire. Maybe the DA was a former real estate broker. Maybe some advice Jack had given my father, some legal caper Dad had entered into as a favor for his old friend, had belly flopped.

Jack gave a little shake of his head, wearing an expression of sorrowful innocence, and maybe I had a speck of intuition, too; for some reason I believed him.

I had to sit down, but I didn't.

I dealt myself a little solace: It would be better than the Oakland jail. Early in his career Dad had handled a few criminal cases, and he had said Santa Rita wasn't so bad, once they learned to put an automatic suicide watch on men waiting for arraignment. He said that the Oakland cells were rape holes, no place for a human being.

"I'll make some tea," I said, and Cindy put her hand over mine, quickly, as though I had said something that shocked her. But it was only sudden gratitude, or her way of saying no thanks.

"Tea would be great," said Jack, and if I hadn't been sure that he simply wanted me out of the room for a while I would have been thankful for his bluff heartiness.

But tea was more my mother's style, what she gave me when I was in bed with a rare episode of flu. Lipton's was folk medicine to Mom, what you drank when you got bad news on the phone. I don't think anyone I know really enjoys the taste. When I had dropped pan lids and tea strainers on the floor, found a tin of Twinings Irish Breakfast that had never been opened, I had water on to boil and a set of questions ready to ask.

I was acting the part of a cool, collected lawyer's daughter. This tea was loose, not the kind that came in bags, and bits of it scattered all over the countertop, all over the floor. Two spoonfuls of tea, or five? I kept the image from my mind, my father sitting on a jail cell cot.

When I wrestled a tray from the cupboard, and had cups, spoons, sugar cubes all arranged, I reentered the dining room. Cindy was on the phone, speaking in a calm, quiet voice, saying their dinner plans had changed, they wouldn't be needing a reservation tonight.

Jack was combing his hair in the mirror over the fireplace. He was going to say that he had to rush off, that he didn't want any tea. I could tell by the I'm-out-of-here lean to his body. One glance at me and he said, "Sure, just what I need." I saw why Dad might enjoy his company.

———

I used to perform what Mom called "community activities," reading to women in a nearby nursing home. Mom donated orchids and bromeliads to the convalescent hospital, the place where her own mother had spent the last weeks of her life. I was probably following my mother's example when I dropped by on Saturday afternoons to read detective novels to white-haired people who shifted in their wheelchairs to catch every clue.

I remember feeling virtuous on the way home from these readings, but only on a honey-sweet, artificial level. On a deeper level, I felt a sickened dismay that a doctor wasn't trying to do more for these frail women. And I was both entertained and frustrated by the mysteries I read. "Start at the beginning of chapter sixteen," a voice would quaver, and I would read all of sixteen, and most of seventeen, enough to recognize that the detective was never going to drag the body out of the creek without going to the village for help. But I never found out who had committed the murder, and I never even knew the names of the patients I read to, careful to keep my voice loud and clear.

I didn't like the way the nurses played up their own good looks and radiant health, wheeling their patients down the hall with such cheer that it seemed disrespectful. I didn't appreciate the way a nurse would beam at a stroke victim nodding off in her chair, "We're getting a head start on our nap, aren't we," as though dying were a jolly business, a sort of summer camp PE.

I couldn't stand the way people pretend that everything is great, when it isn't. I would have called it hypocrisy, but standing there, splashing tea on the coffee-table books. I couldn't blame any of us for putting on an act. I got some paper towels from the kitchen, moving fast, as though the most serious crisis confronting humanity was the terrible problem of tea stains.

Dad would be advising his fellow inmates on how to beat their DUI raps. He'd be drawing up petitions, wills, playing five-card draw. He'd come out of the county jail with after-dinner stories to last a lifetime.

When I asked, finally, what crime my father was accused of committing, Cindy sat with one finger making a dimple in her cheek, as though I had spoken in Sanskrit, and Jack took a slurp of tea still way too hot.

"It's complicated," he said, his eyes on Cindy, as though to get her okay to say more.

"They say he'll be disbarred," said Cindy, her voice vague and almost inaudible, like a talk show left on in another room.

My mind jumped this way and that, eager to twist this statement into something worth celebrating. To be stripped of your license to practice law was a disaster much worse than a weekend eating jailhouse jello.

Jack said, "He's accused of defrauding his clients."

Mom took one look at me and said, "What's wrong?"

Maybe because I was home early, maybe because she had seen Jack's profile in the red Jaguar as he dropped me off. Maybe because I set my gym bag carefully in the bottom of the hall closet and didn't sling it onto the couch the way I usually did. The Jaguar purred away up the street, one of those quiet cars you can hear for a long distance.

Her voice steel quiet, she asked, "What did he do?"

I took my time arranging myself on the sofa, determined to say nothing about any of this to Mom. Jack had not talked much on the drive except to tell me not to sweat this, as though a slangy, casual approach would give me peace of mind. He did add, as he pulled over to the curb, "Cops love reading lawyers their rights."

But I wondered if news about Dad's arrest had been on the ra-dio—Mom doesn't watch much TV. Or if the grapevine of Mom's friends had flashed word that Harvey Chamberlain was marched in handcuffs down the front steps, away from his new bride. Did they use plainclothes cops, or uniforms? When they told him he had a right to remain silent, I wonder if he lifted his eyes from the driveway, the front lawn, to shame them with a smile.

Mom had Polaroids of tropical flower arrangements spread out on the rosewood side table, proteas and ginger blossoms, and classical guitar tinkled in the background, the sort of music she stands in line to hear in concert. But when she saw I wasn't talking, she snapped the remote to shut down the Bose sound system and brushed the pretty flower pictures into a pile with the side of her hand.

"Talk to me, Bonnie," she said, and even when I understood the impression she had, and wanted to reassure her, I still couldn't make a sound.

"If he messed with you—" Mom has bursts of articulate language, but she fades out when she's upset. Her web page is almost all pictures, anthuriums and pink-fruited bananas, not nearly enough text.

"Jack didn't do anything," I said, sounding like he had. I studied the way the toe of my tennis shoe scuffed and smoothed the nap of the carpet.

"What happened?"

I was surprised at how the sounds came out, distorted by my feelings, and I knew Mom couldn't make out a word. But she was a little mollified, half-convinced that Jack hadn't overstepped decency in the front seat of his XJ6. She came over and sat next to me, and right beside me, knee to knee, waiting companionably for me to recover enough to talk, but not pressing, not reassuring me, because by now she knew she didn't have a clue what was wrong.

"They took Dad," I said.

Mom sat with her wise-cat expression and heard everything, everything I knew. I paced up and down, blowing my nose and telling her Dad would sue the County of Alameda for false arrest, and she kept the same attitude, her arms folded easily, letting me wind down.

"Your father will deal with this," she said, after my energy had spun itself out and I was seated again, on the floor with my back to the sofa. "He can take care of himself," she added, but she said this like it was a character flaw.

"I know it," I said, aware that we were having a serious disagreement, even though our words seemed to follow the same path.

She fed some silence into the conversation, the way you feed a fireplace with kindling. "You need to think about us," she said.

I was very close to telling her that life did not consist of making sure all the root fungus in the East Bay has been gamma-rayed to death.

"You need to think about *you*," she said.

I used minimal force, but I couldn't keep my voice steady. "Don't you have any compassion at all?"

I knew, as soon as I had spoken, that I was close to challenging Mom in a way she would never tolerate. She would get up and leave the room.

"Think about your own future, Bonnie. Close your mouth, and take a breath, and think."

I spoke with care. "It's a vendetta. The DA is out to get him."

"Maybe you're right," she said. She went to the side table and sorted her flower snapshots, like a game of solitaire.

Maybe. I couldn't believe what I was hearing.

"It's a real embarrassment for Cindy," she said. She snapped a rubber band around her Polaroids.

"They hauled him away? Your *dad?*" said Denise.

Hauled was a typical Denise verb. Things were always getting stuck, busted, ripped off in her local dialect.

"You make it sound like it would make more sense if my mom got arrested," I said.

"Your mom would make a good crook," said Denise.

"That's a nice thing to say," I responded, feeling no desire to laugh.

"She knows how to keep her mouth shut."

I didn't say, Maybe you should take lessons.

I could hear Denise kicking clothes and shoes off her bed, clearing a place to sit down. My own room was organized, in a fuzzy-logic way. A picture of the first female Olympic champion, Charlotte Cooper, cocked her racket beside a blow-up of Rowan working in the Rockies, cradling a boom mike. I rarely visited Denise's room, not wanting to scale the piles of rubble.

"But your *dad*. It doesn't make any sense," Denise said.

"I know it."

"I mean, in order to defraud his clients he would have to withhold payments from them, for example, right?" Denise was tossing things, soft thuds.

"Clients pay lawyers," I said, "not the other way around."

"Some of the people my dad has working for him," said Denise in her husky monotone, "you absolutely would not believe."

Rowan wasn't home. They have one of those professionally recorded answering messages, a telephone company sort of voice that says that none of the Beals are available right now. I couldn't leave the message I wanted, that my father was in a county correctional facility. I asked Rowan to give me a call, sitting there fingering the plush box that held the pearl.

Mom knocked and put her head in once, just before I snapped out my light. "Myrna's in my room, I forgot to tell you."

Mom has a polyester shoe organizer in her closet, two dozen pockets for pumps, sandals, walking shoes, go-aheads, mukluks, handmades, flats, heels, ninety percent of them shoes she has worn once. Myrna had carried each kitten all the way to this new closet, and now she was ensconced in Mom's old file boxes.

Mom keeps her financial archives here, records going back to the days of the marriage, three steel boxes with latches and locks. Myrna had her back against one of the boxes, FIREPROOF in red letters.

CHAPTER

SIXTEEN

Sometimes a bed is a trap, the sheets a tangled net. I kicked, sweating, tearing the blankets from my body. I was afraid to search my scalp, afraid to press in on my head, sure the skull cap would be fragmented, my hand covered with warm strawberry jam.

I had worked my way through the Dimond Pharmacy vial, and I was down to my last three codeine. I cat-footed into the bathroom, tossed down the medicine with a swallow of water, and stood without turning on the light, wondering what it's like, lying in a jail bunk.

Back in my bedroom, I closed my eyes, groping for the lamp switch. I pushed it, and the light dazzled me, even with my eyes tight.

Pearls come in hues. You can't see the variations at first. Only when you hold one in the creases of your hand and really look. Some pearls are pink blushed, others a soft blue. The gift Dad had given me swung back and forth on its fine gold chain, luminous, the color of a vein just beneath the skin.

To my surprise, Dad had not changed the message on his answering machine on his return from Hawaii. "This is Harvey!" he said, like it was great news, stop the presses, the message he had recorded the day he brought the Panasonic home from Circuit City. I thought Cindy would have recorded a new greeting. "Hello, Cindy," I singsonged into the phone. I added that I was just checking in, aware more than ever what a peculiar, solitary conversation it is, talking to a machine.

Mom had torn the page out of the newspaper, a big ad for pickup trucks, a smiling auto with hands and feet holding up a CREDIT PROBLEMS? sign. She had left the entire page draped over a bowl of wooden Indonesian apples.

My hand reached for it then fell back to my side.

In the end, even though I didn't want to read it, I did, in a few heartbeats. "Grand Jury Slams Eastbay Att'y." No picture, just news of an indictment, a charge of grand theft and fraud, the state bar association commenting how seriously it took the fiduciary conduct of its members. I knew from past interviews with sports reporters how much gets left out of a news story. It said nothing about my father being in custody.

His name wasn't in the headline, although it was printed three times within the news column. Most of the people I knew wouldn't read page nineteen of the Saturday newspaper.

Mom was outside, beyond the pool, near the fishpond, talking on the phone. She has four large white and gold carp, living submarines that nose the tendrils of green scum, mouthing it like very old men. It's one of the reasons she's cautious about loving a cat, sure that Myrna is going to wrestle one of these whales onto the patio. Mom saw me and her expression softened, but we didn't speak, sending each other reassurance across the leaf-flecked surface of the swimming pool.

What was I going to say to him when we met? *Hi, Dad, too bad about your trouble with the cops*? My mother might recommend the silent hug, heartfelt but free of definition. But I didn't know how Dad was going to carry this off. *Hi, Champion, I'm suing Alameda County.*

I used to read comics in the Sunday paper and wish I could draw and ink my own, about a cat who said smart things about the life around it. *Bonnie's going to need some antacids and maybe even some Immodium*, my cartoon cat would be thinking today. I think what I liked most about comics was the way every moment was separate from the others, in its own neat box.

I pushed the metal doors to the academy pool. They are heavy, and you have to lean into the push bars with your full weight. I didn't look toward the deep end of the pool, or the tower.

Miss P was teaching a handful of little kids how to use a kickboard. Little heads, little splashes, feet kicking, kicking from one side of the pool to the other in the shallow end. You learn like that, hanging onto a flat floatation device, until you can freestyle, and you can't remember a time when you couldn't swim.

I sat, arms crossed over my front, remembering my tapes on

how to attain inner peace, deep breath in, deep breath out. It's all breath, one of my tape instructors says. Come what may, you keep breathing.

Even so, the echoed voices and the splashing cheerfulness made it hard to sit there. I've seen the videos, infants swimming like puppies, pearls of air leaking from their smiles, but we forget and have to learn it all over again. If Miss P was surprised to see me, she didn't show it, tweeting her whistle, clapping her hand, calling, "Straight legs, Angelina! Straight!" miming it, standing there holding an invisible kickboard, kicking one leg. Miss P can't fake her feelings. Her eyes were alive, curious.

I got up and slipped a photocopy of the release form into her hand, like a spy delivering a letter of transit. She shook it open, but didn't look at it until she had blown a whistle and the class hung on the side of the pool, wet, smiling faces. Even then she only read it long enough to register my name and the doctor's signature.

Mom says it's all in the legs, and for Mom I think it is. She's tall, and built for power rather than grace. I swim with everything, my entire body. Every part of the anatomy surges through the water, and if you start thinking *My shoulders are too square, I should lock my knees,* you're doing it wrong.

When the class was dismissed, Miss P told the mommies what a wonderful bunch of little fish they were, and I let myself get up from the bench and pad over to the water, giving the quaking surface a swipe with my toes. Miss P plucked a nose clip off the wet concrete without bending her knees.

Miss P waited, watching me. I was going to do a flat dive, the easiest dive in the world, but instead I lowered myself, hitching down into the water, and let go. I stroked across, side to side, and did a few underwater short laps.

I climbed from the water and trailed the wet all the way along the concrete, all the way over to the tower. I swung my arms, worked my shoulders. I was trembling, sure I'd gray-out and collapse.

Chrome has no color. It reflected the arena, warping it, my hand approaching distorted, a fleshy polyp extending toward the rail. Hesitating.

I put my hand on it, forcing myself. I wrapped my fingers around the chrome, the bright surface flawed here where passersby touched it, hanging on to it, looking up to count the steps.

Higher, where no one but the divers climbed, the chrome was pristine. The rail is never as cold as you expect it to be.

I couldn't stand the way the metal got warmer under my hand.

Miss P tugged at the door, the same door the paramedics had trundled through that afternoon. I wanted to call out to her. The metal barrier made a resounding steel thud.

Miss P could still hear me if I called out. She would be right here—I knew she was listening, in her office with the clipboard, sitting there, aware. Maybe right on the other side of the door, giving me time.

By now the surface was going slack, the ripples and chop from the children gradually slowing, the racing lanes in the bottom of the pool straightening, clarifying, almost geometrically exact. One bare foot on the bottom step of the tower, and all I could think was—how dry the step is, the sandpapery surface harsh under the ball of my foot. I didn't climb—I just closed my eyes.

The cut in my head throbbed.

CHAPTER

SEVENTEEN

"How'd it go?" Miss P said, standing beside her desk. Her working space is a heap of schedules, pamphlets, her in/out tray loaded with sports catalogs still in their see-through envelopes. A first aid kit had popped open, elastic bandages and a cot splint.

I was tugging on the beret I had begun to accept as a fashion accessory, a part of my permanent costume. I looked pretty good in it. My street clothes were sweat pants today, and the kind of ancient, predivorce shirt of my father's that Mom wears to hose down the fishpond.

"It went okay," I said.

I wanted to swallow my tongue, turn myself inside out.

"I'm sorry," I said.

She took the cap off a tube of lip balm, applied a little. "You did the best you could."

"Monday," I said. I added, "It'll be harder and harder, the longer I put it off."

She sat. She said nothing, finding a place on her desk for the tube of lip moisturizer.

"Monday—I promise."

Miss P leaned forward in her chair. "In the old days I would have told you to go back in there, suit up again, and drop your body off the top of that tower."

I nearly said, I'd do it—go ahead.

Miss P leaned back in her chair. "Is anyone pressuring you?" she said at last.

"My mom never nags me about working out," I said. That's what we called it: doing back three-and-a-half somersaults with a difficulty rating of 3.3. "Working out," like it was sit-ups and a jog around the track.

"Do I pressure you?"

"Sure. You tell me not to dive when my brain is seeping out of my head."

She let herself laugh quietly and segued into, "The Pacific Coast Invitational at Stanford . . ." She turned to her wall calendar, a vast, paper tablet scrawled with red and black marker, circled appointments. She lifted the calendar page up so we could both see September, fierce red stars marking the date, weeks from now. She let July fall back into place. "If you aren't ready—" She made her hands open like a book, closed them. "I heard about your father."

I took a moment. I wanted my life in neat compartments, Miss P in one comic strip, my father in another. "He'll be okay."

"How about you?" she said.

I couldn't talk.

"Platform diving isn't your entire career," she said. "You have family concerns, you have plans to take up medicine, make a contribution to society. . . ." She let her voice drift into what she thought was an agreeable tone of promise.

"You're saying I can't do it."

"I'm saying you don't have to."

I had trouble meeting her gaze.

"You're wondering why I'm not tough, like I used to be. The legendary Miss P."

I was a little embarrassed. Her nickname was rarely acknowledged by her—it was always *Miss Petrossian*.

"It's actually not a bad form of motivation," she was saying, "the manipulative approach. Make the athlete see that it's all up to her, while the coach looks on from a great height, noble, long-suffering."

"Psychology."

"If you can't make the Pacific Coast Invitational, for sure you'll miss Seattle, and there won't be any Goodwill Games, no pre-Olympic Trials—"

The invitational was being held at Stanford in the fall. I told myself not to worry about something so far in the future, but Miss P always had next year's calendar already on the wall, scribbled notes on weekends a year away.

"That's all right, if that's what you want," Miss P said, putting a paper clip into its box. "Just don't lie to yourself. Every hour that goes by and you aren't working, there are competitors out there in Denver and Salt Lake City and El Centro relieved to hear it. Because they're hard at work right now, Bonnie." She gave me some silence. Then she said, "And you aren't."

"Subtle," I said.

She was studying me, trying to read my expression. Dad always said, look them right between the eyes. "I'm going to tell you something I don't want you to discuss with anyone. This is just between you and me."

I waited.

Miss P likes sappy movies, the kind Mom likes, *The Sound of Music, ET*. One of her favorite movies was about a dog and a cat and a pig who traveled three hundred miles through raging rivers and snowbound hell to find their owners. "I'm starting to consider early retirement," she said.

I was glad she kept talking—I wasn't ready to make a sound.

"What gets harder is caring about scores and wondering what coach is deploying what computer program to teach center of gravity and angle of descent."

I kept quiet, letting my emotions rise to the surface and sink.

"I want you to see that life is more than endurance conditioning," she said, "and one-half twist layouts."

"But you still care," I said.

"Do I?"

For a few heartbeats we just looked at each other.

"My attitude isn't the point. I'll tell you what matters."

At last the conversation was on solid, familiar ground.

"If *you* care, Bonnie," she was saying. "If *you* still want to dive, the first thing you do on Monday is run three miles. You come here, nine o'clock, and we start you off on the springboard."

"The springboard!" I protested.

"You're too proud for that?"

Swimming I could handle. Maybe I could talk her into letting me swim laps all morning Monday. Maybe I could take up swimming, the two-hundred-meter breaststroke, and be realistic about my future.

I was going to say that my father was facing his arraignment on Monday. I couldn't possibly be here.

"I heard you up again in the night," said my mother from the dining room.

She doesn't mind holding a conversation with someone she can't see. She'll talk to a closed door, right at you, or through earphones. It was the next morning, after a night of bad dreams.

"I wake up a lot," I said.

I was slicing a banana. The banana sections looked like primitive coins.

"Why are you eating it like that?" Mom demanded, bustling through the kitchen.

I said something about it being good practice in lab technique. She had a folder marked "Immigration Service" in her hand. An employee had been using the Social Security number of a deceased cousin. She would spend the morning selecting letter formats on her word-processing menu: Business Letter, Personal Letter, Death Warrant.

I had been wondering what role she would adopt: distant but still caring ex-wife, indifferent, nosy. She had opted this morning for the frantic, business-as-usual ploy she used when a cat has died or an unexpected envelope has arrived from the IRS. She said, as she hurried off to the Spartan shelves and drawers of her home office, "I forgot to tell you—there's a postcard for you, from Georgia. Under the wooden fruit."

A sweeping panorama, a beach with gigantic driftwood, the ocean-cured logs of the north coast. "Thinking of you, Egg Head!" she had written in her graceful, feminine hand.

"I called her last night and told her about your father," Mom said.

I asked what Georgia had said.

"She's worried about you," Mom said. "She always said you and your father are like this," she added, holding up two fingers side by side.

Georgia once said the pattern of seeds in a slice of banana look like a monkey's face. My mom says the Man in the Moon looks like a rabbit eating cabbage. I had a piece of rye toast for breakfast, sliced banana, and a glass of pineapple juice.

I gave Rowan a call, knowing the Beals were probably gone for the weekend. But to my surprise Mrs. Beal answered, and said that they had heard about my father's troubles and that they had every sympathy. That was the way she expressed it, making this all sound historical, the Time of the Troubles.

Mrs. Beal has the most wonderful voice on the phone, it melts all opposition. "But you have to come over," she protested. Or maybe she has the gift, knowing what the caller needs to hear.

Mrs. Beal's parents were always appearing in the society pages, fund raisers for the ballet. Mr. Beal's family used to own a company that manufactured environment controls for airplanes—the mechanisms that allow aircraft flying through cold and lethally thin air to turn the atmosphere into warm, breathable gas. Mr. Beal's scuffed hiking boots and loose-fitting plaid shirts were made to order, and their driveway always had brand new cars spattered with mud.

I wondered what they fed you Sunday morning in a county jail.

Mrs. Beal opened the door wearing a sleeveless T-shirt and showing a smile of perfect teeth, the kind you capture after years of orthodontia. She's a size eight and buys clothes already faded, carefully tailored rips at the knee. "Bonnie!" she cried, and I was a survivor, home from a war.

"You're just the one we need," said Mr. Beal.

"I keep telling Dad you're the most resilient person I know," said Rowan, offering me a plate of corn muffins.

"Resilient," I echoed. The Beal family doesn't say you look "good." They say you look "top-hole."

Rowan at once lowered his eyes. For a bright, earnest guy he is easy to embarrass. "I mean—full of life," he said.

"Is *that* what I'm full of?" I said, to laughter all around. Good old Bonnie, keeping her sense of humor. Sometimes I thought that despite their ever-warm welcome, Rowan's parents preferred one of his other girlfriends, the mature sophisticate with long, glossy hair, off to Washington D.C. or Paris to visit her uncle the ambassador.

My dad likes Rowan, always showing him how to lay down a perfect bunt, choking up on the bat, and how to get loose before racket ball, stretching, getting those thigh muscles, the adductor longus, the adductor magnus, ready for action.

Rowan calls his father by his first name, Bill, and his Mom is called Bev by everyone, and while I played along, I was, privately, a little uncomfortable with this casual way of addressing parents.

"Are you ready, Miss Chamberlain?" said Mr. Beal. He had a manly little dimple in each cheek, Thomas Jefferson with short hair.

We drove in a Land Rover so new the gearshift knob had a plastic hood like a shower cap. Pigeon droppings already splotched the hood.

The Pacific rarely confronts broad, gentle beaches in Northern California. The land stretches, blackberry and tawny scruff grass. And then it ends, a cliff, a twenty-meter drop to rocky rubble, and the rinse and shrug of the surf.

I didn't know what sort of trek we had in mind, carrying my part of the gear and the two thermoses—French roast and cranberry juice. Mr. Beal carried the nerve center of the sound equipment in a backpack, and Rowan and I scouted ahead with mike booms, a few lengths of aluminum poles that telescoped into each other. When a casual misstep had me lurching into Rowan, neither of us minded.

The wind tufted the dunes into brief scatterings of sand; the dune grass whispered in the breeze. The air was crisp, the sun warm, kneading through my sweatshirt. Rowan was going on about the charms of a den of coyote pups they had captured with the sort of shotgun mike spies use, and how you could hear each yip as the little teeth of the playful creatures took fun bites out of each other.

I could imagine my father's voice, what he said on one of our visitations, as the divorce became final. We sat on lawn furniture in his new garden, before the white gravel and the bamboo, before the gardener whose tastes had been celebrated in *Sunset Magazine*. Georgia wandered among the stands of wild fennel, and if you didn't know her you would think she wasn't listening.

Dad's landscape in those days had been dry dirt and milkweed, and a cord of firewood snaked over by morning glories. His new house was three stories, with a billiard room and four walk-in closets, a skylight in the master bedroom, and an armed-response security alarm.

Dad pointed out where his sand garden was going to be, a white empty expanse you could rake into different patterns. He showed me where the river gravel would shape a path through fluttering, decorative grasses.

"And we'll put in a swimming pool," he said, "with a hot tub,

Jacuzzi, twelve-foot deep end." He touched me, on my hand, the way he does when he is describing an intercepted pass, a wild throw from center field, trying to pass his enthusiasm like an electric current.

"What is happening now doesn't change the way I feel about you," he said. He turned, speaking toward the shifting, swaying stalks of fennel. "It alters nothing about my feelings for my two girls," he said.

He touched my hand again, and rested his fingers there when he added, "It doesn't change the two of us."

CHAPTER

NINETEEN

It was a long walk, the hike to the sea elephants. I imagined my father avoiding eye contact with tattooed skinheads on his way back from breakfast. I imagined the locker-room echoes of the jail. I wished I could send him a mental picture of the scrub jay chattering in the cypress.

"You haven't reviewed the larger implications of this sort of activity," I was saying, talk as a kind of game I play to keep my mind busy. Maybe I wanted to keep convincing Rowan that I was as smart as his traveling debutante, the one who won prizes in calculus.

"Like what?" Rowan played along, placid as a horse.

The Beals are under contract with Microsoft to expand the Sounds of Nature software. I could easily perceive the fun it would be for a kid in the inner city to double-click on the cow icon and hear a cow moo. But what would happen if the Beals failed to get a sound bite of a killdeer, a bird that lives in the flat marshes in the Bay Area? As a result, when Microsoft decided to issue the next edition of their encyclopedia, the company would omit mention of the killdeer altogether.

The menu of creatures offered would be limited to the animals who had made the Top One Hundred. And animals that didn't make any noise at all, the hermit crab, the lawn moth, would be absolutely overlooked. Rowan agreed that this was very true and a real deficiency in the whole idea of sound-replicated nature.

"You're creating a skewed universe," I said.

His eyelashes were blond in the sunlight.

I added, "I'm not annoying you, am I?"

He laughed.

"Carry on," said Mr. Beal approaching from behind, upbeat but impatient, an army officer wishing the army was all male.

Sea elephants smell funny, even at a distance. They smell like decay, rotting chicken skin, garbage left too long under the sink. They didn't smell bad individually. We nearly stumbled on a living sofa, a finned mammal with doe-like eyes, and she nosed the air in our direction with an air of drowsy courtesy. But the crowd of male sea elephants elbowing up and down the beach in the distance needed to have its locker-room cleaned.

I knew that once the microphones were in place, conversation would enter a cease-fire, so I asked, keeping my voice low, "What would you do if your father got arrested?"

"There isn't much you can do," said Rowan.

"How would you feel?"

"My father gets arrested every now and then," said Rowan. Somehow I had forgotten this, misfiled it in a part of my mind. I could not associate the Beals with criminal conduct.

"The government trucks carry radioactive isotopes," Rowan said. "Right through the streets. They go past schools and Laundromats where they could have an accident. Bend a fender and spill plutonium all over the intersection. My father gets together with a Sierra Club spin-off, a group called Atomic Abstinence. They picket the nuclear research lab in Livermore, the Port of Oakland." Rowan shrugged: Parents, what can you do?

I hate coming out with such a bare question. "He's been in jail?" I asked, keeping my voice down, Mr. Beal intent on untangling his earphones.

"Overnight, once or twice. When it comes to sentencing, the judge orders him to do community service. He goes around playing the voices of the carnivores for school kids."

"It's important for children to learn all about hunting and killing," I said. What I wanted to say was, Doesn't it bother you?

"Dad says he looks pretty good," said Rowan lightly, "in a county jail jumpsuit."

He must have read the trouble in my eyes. Rowan put his arm around me, enclosing me. "Don't worry, Bonnie."

I wanted to joke: Okay, whatever you say.

"Your dad didn't do anything wrong," he said, his lips at my ear. Sometimes I'm self-conscious about my earring hole, thinking I should go back to wearing jewelry.

"The courts make all kinds of blunders," Rowan was saying. "During one of my dad's protests the cops arrested a mailman, gathered him in with the protesters. He was just following his route, delivering mail."

I managed a creaking what-do-you-know laugh.

"The law is really stupid, Bonnie."

Maybe Rowan didn't realize that if the courts could make tiny mistakes, they could also make a really gigantic one and put an innocent man in prison.

"If it's all right with you two," said Mr. Beal, in a half-whisper. Worry lines had appeared in his forehead, the equipment all set up, the digital recorder he had bought in Japan. This was a new Mr. Beal, one I had not seen, the pro at work, and I was almost relieved to see how impatient he was, eager to get Rowan in place with the microphones. I had wondered if the Beals communicated perfectly with each other, every blessed minute.

Rowan put a finger to his lips but motioned me to come on. I tiptoed by Mr. Beal, sure he would snap something at the two of us. But Mr. Beal had that otherworldly expression people wear when they are listening through earphones, and Rowan and I took our places just ahead, on the ridge of a dune.

I had not been aware of any danger, but now I put my hand to my chest.

My body perceived the threat. Not just my eyes and ears. My entire nervous system tingled. Sea elephants basked just a few meters away. Most of the animals were in an advanced state of molt, tattered fur lofting and spinning from their bulk. The blown tatters of skin felt artificial, like nylon. I tucked a triangle of fur into the hand pockets of my sweatshirt. I would show it to Dad. I would bring my father here, soon, next week.

He would love the massive athleticism of the young males, each the size of a Buick, crashing through the surf, plundering the sand, heaving upslope. Almost every individual hulk rose up from time to time to spar with a neighbor. Each sea elephant had a boxing-glove-size swelling on his nose, and he punched and blocked with this single fist. Sparring partners ascended together, rising high from the crusty sand, and their mutual weight would send them toppling, crashing into the sea foam.

Dad would admire the way Rowan sat, eyes narrowed, catching every belch and chuckle, perched on the ridge, holding the microphones aloft on a glittering aluminum T. He looked my way and lifted his eyebrows: Quite a noise.

I rolled my eyes in agreement, like I was used to this. When I looked back at Mr. Beal he flashed me encouragement with his eyes. We were trespassing, I knew, stealing something, close to these massive animals so we could lift their voices from the air. We did no harm, but I felt the hush of a thief.

The sound was guttural, tenor and bass, growling, yammering, and sometimes one elephant seal would roar. It was the kind of thunder that must have awakened people in villages centuries ago, wide-eyed, gasping: Was it only a dream?

CHAPTER

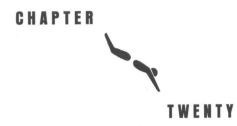

TWENTY

Well before dawn the summer before this, the telephone had startled me awake. I thrashed, struggling to find the clock radio, thinking it was time to get up and run my miles.

I picked up the telephone at last, desperate to silence the source of the noise. "Go outside in the backyard," my father's voice was saying, "and look up at the sky, Champion. Don't ask, don't talk, just do what I say, and call me back. Do you hear me? Are you there?"

I was sleep-silly, three-thirty in the morning. "Okay," my voice said, like a rasp from the tomb. He hung up, and I sat there in the bedding. It's hard for me—some people are brisk before breakfast. I crawl.

Mom had bought me a cute phone, mock antique, fake ivory and gilt, a rococo instrument a gangster's girlfriend might use. The problem was you couldn't take it anywhere. I staggered into the bathrobe I had long ago outgrown, the frilly one I rarely wore beyond the bedroom, and I mouse-footed my way through the kitchen, outside.

Neighborhood quiet surrounded me, a last cricket, a steady rush and hiss of freeway sound. I tilted my head. We don't get much of a night sky in the Bay Area. Summer clouds, winter rain, city lights, smog. You can sometimes look up and catch the moon. And if you let your night vision develop you can see a few of the more brazen stars, point to point in the smoggy dark.

But I expected what I saw: not much, a few stalwart stars, a slender piece of moon going tan as it approached the western horizon. I was more concerned about not falling into the pool and not tripping over the sprinkler at the end of the hose. Still, I kept looking. Dad was watching with me, in his bamboo-and-gravel garden a couple of miles away.

A flash across the sky. Another. Like flaws in my own vision, glints that weren't there, too fast. I lay down flat on the dewy crab grass.

It was a meteor shower, flicking chips of light that arced across the sky. I could almost sense my father watching with me.

I stayed like that until dawn and finally fell asleep there, curled up on the wet grass. Mom approached me in the sun glow, her features set, a woman afraid to make a sound. We made it a joke later, the expression on her face, but we both knew what she had been thinking, my body flung there on the tough, prickly grass.

The Beals dropped me off late that afternoon, sunburned and full of stories, shouting over the ragged, metallic jazz Mr. Beal loves to play at full volume, saxophones and anguished trumpets. They had a good laugh over the story of Rowan running full-out from a cougar at Tamales Bay, the cat wondering if Rowan was lunch.

"That was really stupid," cried Rowan over a drum solo. "You never run from a predator."

When I left the car Rowan snapped out of his nature-happy routine and reached for my hand. "Everything's going to be all right, Bonnie," he said. His father waited at the steering wheel, gazing off at the street, keeping time to the music with tiny movements of his head.

"Everything," Rowan said, getting out of the car to hold me.

I couldn't say anything that would keep him there in the gathering twilight.

"This is a piece of sea elephant skin," I said.

Mom fingered the triangle of fuzzy polyester-like fur. She said, "Yuck," but with something like wonder.

I was glad to reenter my mother's solar system. Her professional life had spilled out of her office, paper clips and envelopes, and she was working at the dining room table. Her hair was gathered back in a shaggy, silvery ponytail, a style that didn't look that good on her.

I gave her a brief verbal postcard, peanut butter and jelly and seagulls. I left out the sunlight in the hair of Rowan's arms, the muscle in his jaw bunching as he chewed.

I put my elbows on the table.

As though sensing my deletion, Mom said, "Rowan and his dad had a good time?"

I wanted her to know that this had been a serious activity, contributing to science and the spread of knowledge. "I like them," I added.

She gave me a thoughtful smile. "I do, too," she said. She let one arm hang, the other draped across the table, a folder of receipts, the sort of paperwork you're required to keep on file for four years. You can only work so long, even to take your mind off trouble.

I hadn't planned to talk, but it happened. I found myself describing my dream and said I was down to antihistamines in the medicine cabinet, hoping they would help me sleep. I told Mom Miss P was thinking of retiring. I told her Miss P was leaving it all up to me. I wasn't supposed to tell anyone that she was thinking of early retirement.

"Smart," said Mom after a short silence.

"She's good at it."

"Are you hungry?" Mom asked, meaning: Did I want to keep talking?

"Not yet," I said.

It got dark before we even noticed none of the lights were on.

Mom's swimming career had burned out in her sophomore year at UCLA, a sprung rotator cuff in her right arm. The coaches drove us *like this*, she would say, showing a fist being shoved into someone. Maybe that's why she stressed that swimming was ninety percent legs, because she had such ruined cartilage in her shoulders. The coaches, she thought, consumed her career, forcing laps when the team was puking water. I knew Mom would love to have me swim competitively, but she wasn't crazy about platform diving. An eavesdropper would have wondered that the subject of my father never came up.

We sat in the dining room running my options, detailing, once again, her past growing up in Victorville in the Mojave Desert, the lights of LA blue on the horizon. Every morning as a girl she used a pool rake to skim off yucca spears and shiny black beetles *this big*, she would say, indicating an insect the size of a blackbird.

"Let the coaches push you around," Mom said, "and they'll kill you."

I called Cindy, and she said the arraignment was set for the courthouse in downtown Oakland, but there was no way to predict any of the details. She said this in a way that told me she was familiar with the world of bail bonds and court calendars, and that I was not.

CHAPTER TWENTY-ONE

I slept pretty well that night. I realized it when I woke a little after four, according to the red digits on the clock radio. It defied logic, my dreamless sleep, because as soon as I was awake the dread hit me, like a power that had been stored up and waiting.

I wasn't going to be able to go through with this. I put both feet on the floor, but did not stand up.

A voice in me said: *Stay here.*

Don't go.

It was damp-warm outside, dark, but too cloudy for meteors. Besides, the annual Perseid shower, the sight of which had so excited Dad that early morning, wasn't due yet. I didn't bother with stretching exercises, just jogged in place on the sidewalk, then kicked into an easy stride, uphill, toward the fading stars.

I was running well when I hit the overpass, the Warren Freeway already packed with traffic I could have easily outpaced. I passed the home where Denise and her parents lived, the au pair girl's cottage nestled among Monterey pines. I used to love running with Denise; she can jog hours without complaint. I had gone out of my way to stop by the iron-spear fence of her front garden, but there was no sign of her.

I took a flash shower, toweled dry, and had milk and egg protein powder, no banana, no toast. Myrna sallied forth to greet the morning and accepted a scratch on her head. Some people think animals are a lot like people. I think they are nothing like us, except that they like attention.

I tossed what I needed into the gym bag. I took the shortest route, but I made myself stop and give my greetings to one of the local terrors, a Great Dane. The beast planted both paws on the cinder-block wall that protected the neighborhood from his wrath and gave a ragged bark, half threat, half hi.

There was no way I was going to be able to do it. I nagged at myself, aware that I was trying to fool myself, and it wasn't working. I was afraid.

One of the custodians was unlocking the arena, whistling a tune. He did not act surprised to see an athlete here so early. He said, "Good morning how are you," in a rush, the words all together, maybe one of those people who understand English but don't like to speak it.

I wondered what happened if you suffered a subdural hematoma in the same place after a recent injury, how much damage it would do, how much permanent harm.

The locker room was dark except for the twenty-four-hour

glow from the coach's booth, where the fire extinguisher and bales of clean towels are stored. The overhead fluorescence stuttered on, slow to wake. The locker room has a strangely yeasty smell, clean cotton and disinfectant. A drip somewhere splashed, *tap tap tap*. My swimsuit did not feel as tight as usual, as though I had lost weight.

Poolside was dry. My feet whispered on the rough surface. I didn't look at the tower as it approached.

CHAPTER

TWENTY-TWO

I once saw a man hit by a car. A hefty Detroit monster, with rust holes where a strip of chrome had fallen away. The man was jogging in place in the middle of the street, the intersection of MacArthur and Fruitvale, and the vehicle brushed him lightly, a kiss. It was only when the man danced to one side and couldn't bring his leg along that we all saw what was wrong.

Maybe in the following minutes I decided to be a doctor. My mother was riveted by the sight, and half-shielded me as the adult world gathered in to bunch its fists and look grimly around, waiting for the ambulance. But I had seen the empty cut of the man's mouth, a gray-haired man dressed in the brightly colored, zip-fronted jogging wear that had been in style then. I heard his angry "Don't touch me!" and I knew as though I had read a computer printout—it didn't hurt yet. The pain would be later. We all knew that, that some miracle of the nervous system stunned him, kept him unmoving.

Or maybe it was during my first eye checkup, Dr. Wong holding a device like a flat spoon over my right eye and telling me to read the numerals in a spot of light that glowed, in a muted way, like a moon. When he peered into the caverns of my eyes with his pinpoint light, I saw the reflected blush of my veins, crooking like the roots of trees. When I gave a laugh of amazement, he said, in his exacting accent, "The smallest blood vessels in your body—some so small they let through only one blood cell at a time!"

I like emptiness, a theater before the crowd, the swimming arena before anyone in the world thought to arrive and slip into the water.

The lines on the pool bottom were exact, perfectly straight. I dipped my toe, slicing the surface of the water, and that entire plain, so calm, quaked outward from my touch. At once, water gurgled in and out of the filter valves, a sound like a dog lapping water very, very slowly. The metal and plastic disks in the poolside, the access vents to the inner plumbing of the pool filter and the pumps, gleamed in the light from the windows high above the bleachers. The Stars and Stripes hung motionless at one end of the arena, beside the water polo team's home/visitor scoreboard. My bare feet made echoing *slap slap* sounds on the concrete.

I walked briskly now, decisively, aware that I should use pumice on the calluses on my heels.

Habit marched me upward, three steps, four. Or perhaps it was a victory, my will asserting itself. Halfway up the tower my nerve failed. My knees locked and I had that bizarre sensation that my knee joints were going to bend backward and render me a sports-medicine freak. I stiff-legged my way higher, not letting myself count the remaining steps.

My pulse flickered in my vision, the retinal net of blood vessels hammering, hammering. Deep breath, I told myself. A long breath, all the way in, head to toe. Breathing belongs to us, Miss P said. Control respiration, you control your soul.

Like so much else wise people say, it is only a little bit true. I steadied myself on the steps, guessing I was more than two thirds of the way up. I looked down. I would have gasped, except that I did not let myself give in to such a sound.

I gripped the chrome rail, left hand, right hand. I wanted to laugh, but couldn't. I had no memory of the tower being so high. A seam in the poolside ran from the edge of the pool and all the way to the bright blue wall, the sort of rubberized seam contractors build into structures in California to make them earthquake resistant. If I weakened and fell from here, I would plummet headfirst.

If I fainted.

The scar in my scalp burned. I ground my teeth and won another step, and another. I began making hectic deals with myself, shouted thoughts, mental bargains. This time I would climb to the top of the steps and then I would rubber-leg down. That was all. My breath shuddered in and out, and to my horror the rail was curving, rounding to its summit. I had reached the top.

I felt betrayed by the stair railing, abandoning me to a nar-

119

row, open flat. But a new railing took up where the ascent rails surrendered, and I clung to the side of the platform without rising to my feet. I stayed on my knees, hobbling forward, hand to hand.

They were like the protective barrier along the side of a ship, I told myself. Solid, firmly welded into place. I played a mental animation for myself, a welder at work, sparks flying. This is steel, I told myself. Anchored. Going nowhere.

A metal crash.

A loud, echoing sound. I would be all right if I didn't move. If I stayed right there and never released my grip.

The sound faded, reverberating, and from far away I heard the tuneful whistle of the custodian. He had been performing some janitorial task, checking the door to make sure it was unlocked, or testing the door's crossbar, going off to get some oil—the thing tended to stick. I let the sweetness of the song he whistled tease me into optimism for a moment. The world was lovely. I could be somewhere else.

I hung on so hard it hurt. But the realization of the exterior world awakened me to the potential that Denise would arrive for her workout, and Charlotte Witt for her sweet, ordinary dives, and all the rest of them, unthinkingly confident. They would see me and wonder, and then turn to each other with whispered understanding. Poor Bonnie, creeping along on the platform.

I crawled a little farther, and then I pulled myself to my feet and stretched first one leg, then the other. I sidled outward, halfway to the edge.

Divers have a favorite place on the platform, an imaginary equator. You know when you reach it, and I was there now. Three steps would bring me to some eighteen inches from the void, and then I would launch my hurdle, the last skipping step—and I couldn't remember how I used to do it. I was like a little girl studying ballroom dancing from a library book, footsteps connected by sweeping dots, none of it making sense.

I had seen beginners like this, cocky seventh graders introduced to the tower for the first time, huffing all the way up, and then balking, avoiding setting foot on this mesa, this slab of emptiness that you could walk out on and disappear. I had glanced up at skinny kids, up there above the pool, and felt a quiet, interior laugh. I would have laughed at myself, at the sight of me like a scarecrow in the middle of the platform.

Miss P says that if you can't dive well, dive badly. I gave the seat of my suit a tug.

What part of our minds makes the decision, on a cold morning: Get out of bed *now*? My arms and legs chose the time. It was a sloppy dive, a front dive from a layout position, my arms outstretched. The sort of dive you see caught in photos, the diver's arms like wings. A classic dive, the athlete face first into the approaching wall, the water.

All the way down I felt my form crumble, my legs falling forward. I was starting to tumble. I rotated my arms to stop the roll, sure I would hit the pool before my form totally dissolved. I didn't. There was plenty of time. I pancaked, back and rump slamming the water.

Michael Cadnum

My body remembered this very well: the artificial aquamarine of the pool bottom, the steely grin of the drain, the wooden pressure in my ears. It hurts, hitting like that. I did a mental assessment, damage control, standing on tiptoe in an almost soundless environment, warped whale-song noises from the inner workings of the pool, and from my own body, holding its breath.

CHAPTER

TWENTY-THREE

The Alameda County courthouse is a chunky white building, like the capitol of a foreign country you can't quite name. In morning light it looks almost pink, a substantial place, surrounded by rivers of rushing traffic. The structure has been made earthquake resistant, its foundation far underground consisting of huge wheels. A jolt and the building will roll, but not crumble.

In theory. The view from the courthouse steps isn't bad, Lake Merritt to the east, and the tall apartment buildings that grace the shore. You pass through a metal detector, and a sheriff's deputy makes you open your purse, your briefcase. I had to pull my beret off and let the deputy dangle it in his fingers, as though he was surprised it didn't keep its shape.

People extend their arms out from their sides, detector wands waved up and around their limbs. You can tell which ones are lawyers, cracking their briefcases, gazing past the security barrier to the bustling figures beyond. Some of the citizens are new to it, though, and they thank the woman holding their car keys out to them on a tray, careful to show no offense.

An arraignment is usually simple. I knew this from war stories of my dad's, from when he first started out defending marijuana dealers and bosses' daughters caught shoplifting. You plead innocent, you post bail, the legal system digests things for a few hours, and, unless you were arrested for butchering a family of five, you go home.

That didn't explain why I was so nervous. "It's just a bad way to start the day, that's what I'm saying," Cindy was explaining. She had gotten a parking ticket right outside the office, just a five minute walk away. "It's an insult, what with everything."

"Think of it as a donation," said Jack, holding open the door for both of us, "to the city of Oakland. Be philosophical."

"It's just a bad way to start, is what I mean," said Cindy.

The man at the gum-and-candy stand in the lobby said, "How's it going?" to Jack, and the lawyer bought himself a roll of Certs. "Anything for either of you?" he asked, peeling money off a roll he kept tidy with a gold clip.

"No sweat about any of this, Bonnie," said Jack as we headed down a corridor. He was dressed in a heather-brown suit with a narrow waist, and a pair of shoes I recognized from Christmas shopping at Nordstrom, hand-lasted, five hundred dollars tied up in footwear.

Just then my ear tickled, a trickle of water from my inner ear, a remnant of the morning's workout. I had done maybe a dozen front dives, and the last three or four were clean entries. I hadn't

tried anything difficult—nothing like a somersault, just the ordinary dives Denise used to perform so well. I left the locker
room in a hurry, before anyone else arrived.

"You need anything?" Cindy asked. She was wearing too
much eye shadow.

"I'll just hang around," I said. I had put on lipstick and fussed
with my eyebrows in the locker room mirror, too.

"You're going to be okay out here?" Jack was asking, like no
one ever leaned against a wall in this particular hallway, unless
you were a witness waiting to be called. Maybe I had tried to
con myself into believing my father would be arraigned in a different variety of courthouse, not this hectic, lifeless place. At
one end of the corridor a string of prisoners linked to each
other, handcuff chained to handcuff, trailed into a doorway. I
had the sickening thought I might catch sight of my father,
shuffling along in an orange jumpsuit. I didn't want my father
to see me here.

"It won't take any time at all," said Jack.

Two hours later Cindy marched into the hall, sorting through
her purse like a cigarette addict. She found a Kleenex and
touched it to her face, chin, and cheek. "They arrested half of
Oakland over the weekend," she said. "Plus someone called in
a bomb threat last Thursday. The bailiffs are pissed off, and
everybody's way behind."

"What does Jack say?"

"He's nonstop on his cell phone, doing business. Nothing

slows him down." She said this like it wasn't a compliment to his character.

Cindy turned to face me, and her eyes searched my face for a moment. Then her hand reached out and touched me, on the side of my head. "Bonnie, honey, don't put yourself through this," she said.

I explained that I didn't want Dad to think I was letting him down.

"Down?" she echoed, latching onto that word like it was the key to my statement. "Nobody has ever said anything about letting people *down*."

Later, during a late lunch, after I gave up on the criminal justice system for a while, I kept thinking about her choice of words, and mine. I sat alone at a counter, a crowd of lawyers and legal secretaries shaking Equal into their coffee. I thought that maybe people in the Midwest used language with a different twist from people in California.

Either she meant that Dad had every faith in me, no question about it, or she meant that I was the last thing on my father's mind right now. I chewed my tomato and tuna sandwich, a pickle and a carrot stick in a basket lined with green paper. I sipped ice water. Or maybe she had some other meaning, something she had not quite meant to say.

I gave up waiting at last, took BART to the Fruitvale station, and rode the bus to my neighborhood, life puttering along, kids with new skateboards, delivery trucks parked along curbs bringing furniture, new glass for broken windows.

"My dad knows a professional killer, a real hit man, and he's been arrested five times and never served a day," said Denise.

It was time for the yearly assault on water weeds in my mother's fishpond. *Please*, Mom had asked, and I was glad to humor her. I had called five times, and there was still no answer at my father's house, only his happy answering machine.

I used a short-handled hoe, and Denise used a trowel, and sometimes the white and scarlet carp would chug slowly past our ankles, touching us with a feathery fin. Denise had never done this before, and I had convinced her what fun it was, giving the fish a better view of life.

Denise wouldn't shut up about the hired gunman, how he talked at parties, like he didn't care what happened to him. Sometimes you know a story isn't true—or is at best an exaggeration—but you don't feel like arguing.

"My dad's an attorney," I said finally. Meaning: Not a professional killer.

"He's a lawyer," said Denise, with an air of casual dismissal. Sometimes Denise doesn't know when to stop talking.

"What does *that* mean?" I asked, unable to keep quiet.

Denise straightened her back, maybe not quite in shape for this. She took her time, picking out her words. "How long was your workout today?" she asked.

"Long enough."

"What did you do, three laps and a shower?"

"I dove off the platform."

"Miss P said she guessed you couldn't come in today."

I kept calm. "Her office was locked, and I didn't leave a note."

"She had me doing reverses today, a pike and a somersault." A pike is when the diver nearly touches her toes, more elegant than a tuck, but less exciting to watch. This drill was not hard, compared with the back three-and-a-half somersault I had long since been able to do. I let Denise see that I didn't mind, continuing to chop at the bottom weeds. After all, I reasoned, she had to gradually take on the more demanding dives. It was only natural.

"If you can't do it, Bonnie, everyone understands," said Denise.

I chopped a stalk of water lily clean through.

"You have to learn not to lie to yourself, Bonnie. It's a criticism I have to make about your family, how they have trouble coming right out and saying anything."

Denise has dark brown hair and dark eyes, and at times like this her features are too close together in the middle of her face. I gripped the short-hoe so hard it hurt my hand.

"I want to help you, Bonnie. If you're afraid, live with it," Denise said. "If your father is a crook, accept it."

I told her to leave.

"I'm not going anywhere, I'm staying right here. I'm being a good friend to you, Bonnie."

I told her to use the side gate, don't bother going through the house.

That night I sat at my desk with a piece of acid-free paper, one hundred percent cotton, the kind Dad recommends for making permanent drafts of a document. A moth sang off the lampshade, then fluttered inside it, a rhythm like nervous fingers in a waiting room. I fingered the gold-nibbed calligraphy pen Dad had given me for Easter a couple of years before. Audrey ran in her exercise wheel, a quiet whirring whisper.

J. T. Breen. B. T. Chamberlain. My middle name is Tyne, my mother's family name. I had been practicing, trying to give my square, compact handwriting the powerful leaps and turns that are evidence of insight and determination.

I wrote the letter carefully, and when I was done I read it aloud. Sometimes you would swear animals know something. Audrey stopped running, her agate-red eyes toward the sound of my voice.

CHAPTER

TWENTY-FOUR

There's a peephole in my dad's front door, a glass pupil about the size of a squirrel's eye. I suppose the builders thought a burglar might show up on the front step and push the doorbell, hoping to be let in.

I sensed movement in the interior of the house, and the little glass hole darkened. Peepholes, with their fish-eye lenses, turn even a harmless visitor into a goofy, swollen cartoon. Maybe I should have waited, I thought, imagining my father asleep in a darkened bedroom.

"He's in the back," Cindy said, as soon as she opened the door. Not hello, not good morning. A hairbrush in one hand, her feet planted, like she didn't want me to come in.

I hesitated in the dining room, smoothing my hair back under the beret, straightening my skirt, a woolen garment with about thirty pleats. Dad had an assortment of plaid mufflers, tartan neckties, and every time he came back from golf in St. Andrew's, he brought me a wool sweater or a skirt, good heavy tweed, but not my style.

My clothes didn't go with the backpack I set in a corner of the dining room, under a work of art I didn't recognize, a blue figure dancing. I made sure my backpack was upright. I didn't want it falling over and crumpling the letter zipped into a side pocket.

"Can I get you anything?" Cindy was asking. It was mid-morning, approaching lunchtime, but I wasn't hungry. I looked a question at her, and she made a minute shake of her head: she didn't want to say. Or maybe she meant: How would *you* be doing—after a weekend in jail?

"Jack got him released by supper yesterday," Cindy said. "Bail was set at two hundred thousand dollars—hardly anything in a case like this. And you know what he told me, the first thing he got home?"

I played along with her, telling her no, I didn't know. I wasn't sure I was ready for a report of jail brutality, and I was wondering how my father had posted such a large amount of cash.

"He said he was taking me to New Orleans, to eat nothing but gumbo."

She said this with pride, but with an undertone of fatigue.

"Gumbo gives him a stomachache," I said.

Dad's backyard had turned out pretty much as he had envisioned it. A Japanese man named Eiichi, an expert in sand and rock, drops by weekly to pick up the slender fingers of bamboo that have drifted onto the sand, one by one, tucking them into his hand.

But that's the trouble: bamboo flutters, ever moving. Even the slightest wind blurs the gentle lines the gardener has combed into the sand. My father's swimming pool was designed by an award-winning pool visionary. It has a charcoal gray bottom, with hewn slate flagstones at poolside. But the back garden is crowded, a Jacuzzi seething quietly, a sauna like a log cabin. Too much, you think, walking out to find a place out of the sun. Too much to look at. There is a putting green off to one side, the grass razored short and firm, a single hole at one end.

Dad stood surveying it all, wearing white slacks and leather sandals, the ones he had custom made in Florence. A golf club, a putter, glittered in his hands. His yellow shirt was so new you could see the folds in it, fresh from the package. I expected him to look a lot different, but he tucked in a loose shirttail, adjusted the crease in his pants, quietly impatient, knocking a ball all the way to the cup.

At one end of the putting green a stone frog is parting his mouth, a little fountain of water playing into a metal bowl. The Santa Rita jail suicide watch means that every fifteen minutes a county officer peers in at each inmate, twenty-four hours a day. My father didn't look weary so much as pale. Dad didn't hear me coming, and then just before I reached his side I made a little coughing noise.

"Champion!" He let the putter fall. But it was one of those moments when you wonder how the hug is going to go, where his chin will fit, where your face will end up, whether to settle for a hug, or maybe to add a kiss as well.

His voice was very quiet, telling me I looked good. He held me tight, and then held me at arm's length, taking in the view of my face.

"Why the sad face, Champ? Look me in the eye."

I *was* looking.

"I kept thinking of you, all the while, Champion," he said, feeling in his voice. "It kept me going, I want you to know that. The image of your face in my mind."

I hate tears, the way they suddenly decide it's time for the show, the dancing waters, and nothing can stop them.

"I know, it's hard," he said, "even for a strong person like you. This is hard for all of us. I want you to be patient with me because I have something to say to you."

"You don't have to tell me anything," I began, but the words came out strangled. Some things I don't want to hear.

He put a *shhh* finger to his lips. "Listen to me. Are you ready to listen?"

I couldn't make a sound.

"Just nod your head. You can do that, right? Move your noggin a little bit for me? There you go, the amazing human head. Good. Now don't talk for a second."

He had used some of the bay rum I had given him for his last birthday, January 3. He had always hated having a birthday so close to the holidays. It had cheated him out of a lot of bikes and electric trains over the years, he used to joke.

"Keep this in your mind, at all times, Bonnie. Remember these words, no matter what you hear, no matter what you read."

My eyes had stopped leaking. The frog fountain was loud, bright peals of water.

He said, "I didn't do any of this."

Before I could protest that he didn't owe me any kind of explanation, he continued, "You can't be still for ten seconds while I tell you the truth." He was gentle, but it kept me quiet, standing right where I was.

He spoke slowly. "What is happening to me, and to my family, is absolutely unjust."

He paused, studying my eyes, how the words hit me.

"I want you to know that," he said. "You think I don't have to come out and say it. It embarrasses you, to hear me say I'm innocent?"

I steadied myself, breath in, breath out.

"I won't remain silent about this, Bonnie. Because there are a few true things in life. Only a few. The sun comes up in the morning. It sets in the evening. The earth is round."

His parents used to make a living delivering trailers up and down California, working out of an asphalt lot in El Cajon. Trailers of every size and purpose, dwelling places on wheels, on-site offices for construction sites, trailers full of equipment for traveling rodeos. The Chamberlains pulled three hundred thousand miles a year, towing someone's rolling stock.

"And one other true thing: and you know what I'm going to say. You know, don't you."

He waited until I gave him a sign with my eyes. He touched the palm of one hand with his forefinger, saying softly, with a deliberate cadence, "I am, in every way, absolutely innocent."

"I know," I said, when I could talk. "I never doubted you."

"Doubted me?" he said, seizing on that one word.

"I never did."

One heartbeat, two, three.

Then he gave me his smile. "Thank you, Champion."

TWENTY-FIVE

I suited up in the locker room. My tweed skirt filled the locker, ten pounds of Highland wool. I poked the folds of cloth carefully into place and got the door latched after a struggle. They were really going to have to work on that leak in the showers, the dripping water like a percussion instrument.

I had envisioned all this, played it out in my mind. But now that I was close to committing act one, scene one, my fingertips were cold. Some musicians and stage-fright stricken actors take beta blockers, chemicals that shut down the anxiety centers of the brain.

I had timed my workout for early afternoon, so Miss P would be there with all the swimmers and divers. I couldn't suppress all the old doubt. It nagged at me, ugly inner voices warning me, as I pushed open the door from the locker room and caught the familiar waft of chlorine and that strange incandescence a swimming pool casts upward into the space that surrounds it.

I caught Miss P in an ideal moment, most of the team sitting at attention on the lower levels of the bleachers while Miss P demonstrated posture, how to stand, how to let you arms hang, full of their own weight and the weight of all your tension. You give your arms a shake, and you lose some of that anxiety, letting it run from your forearms, through your fingers, out into the air.

I kept walking, in no particular hurry, letting them all get a good look.

Miss P called my name, and Denise looked up from examining her toenails. It would be wrong to say I was unafraid. The old feeling was there, but now I had another feeling, a stronger one, to set against it.

Denise had lost a little too much weight, maybe clocking too many hours on the rowing machine with her personal trainer. Miss P believed in cross-training, practicing other sports to stay in shape, but I always wondered if Denise threw herself with too much gusto into everything that came along. Her father had been right to fire the tennis pro, the one with curly hair all over his shoulders.

Denise almost left her place on the bleachers. She nearly called something to me, a smudge of weariness under each eye. The new dives were taking the glow out of her. Her white bathing cap perched on the bleacher beside her, the top of a skull.

As I passed her I mouthed, "It's all right." And I meant it. She stared right back with cautious disbelief, maybe because in her family people resolve their disagreements by giving each other the finger and taking near-miss swipes at each other's heads.

"Bonnie!" It was Miss P at her most commanding tone, a chilling sound, magnified by the hollow reverberation of the arena. "Get over here!"

I climbed the steps of the tower.

I had told my father once about the imaginary line in the platform, where the diver feels her dive should begin. How when the feet touch this place in the cold, sandpapery surface of the platform, the diver feels strangely at home. "*Querencia*," Dad called it when I described it. "The place in the bull ring *el toro* makes his own. Once he finds that place, he'll kill all comers."

I reached the top step and found the place in the platform where my dives begin.

I got good altitude, and did a back somersault.

The water is always a surprise the first dive of the day. Warmer than you expect, or—usually—colder. My nostrils burned, and the sterile taste of the water seeped through my lips. I let my breasts and tummy glide along the pool bottom, and then I let my body loft toward the light.

I broke the surface.

It had not been a very good dive. Just one somersault. Not the worst dive ever done, but far from my usual, my knees bent, my body at an angle. The splash had been bad, the water still simmering from the impact.

There were calls of encouragement, and Denise was clapping, but they were extras in my own personal movie, a part of the living wallpaper. They could have been cheering in Gaelic,

Miss P, too, although she put her hands on her hips and assumed an aspect of approval: Go ahead, keep going.

As though I paid them any attention.

The second time off the tower I managed two somersaults, and I felt the whisper of air around the platform as my head almost kissed. I entered the water with about as much grace as an office chair.

I pulled myself out of the water, streaming and splashing all the way, and smoothed my hair back away from my eyes, pulling it tight with my hands, so tight my eyes slanted and my eyebrows stretched. I tugged the seat of my suit, and gave my nose a pinch, checking for excess fluid from my sinuses.

My fellow athletes and the few straggling spectators all froze in place, like a photograph. I mountaineered my way up the platform again, and drove every thought, every doubt, from my mind.

But some shadow must have lingered. I completed a back three-and-a-half somersault, with a perfect tuck. My entry was not so good, though, my feet out of position. You dive with your whole body, and your whole heart, and if there's a little question in your mind, it shows up somewhere, even in your toes.

My fourth dive was textbook, from top step to pool bottom, and I let the momentum carry me along underwater, wanting this private silence, the pressure at my eardrums, the clunk and gurgle of the pool valves. Even when the pool water appears unruffled and without current, it isn't. The pumps are at work, under the surface, pulling water through the filters.

An injured athlete has an invisible spotlight around her, and the other teammates stand aside, giving that extra space. They mean no harm. But when your recovery has been established, that aura is gone, and you are yourself again. Hands reached for me, pounded my shoulders, and Miss P grinned and shook her head, in her best I-knew-you-could manner. But I didn't join the team on the bleacher seats. I was on act two of the drama I had in mind. I skimmed across the concrete, into the locker room.

I was quick to shower and pull myself into my clothes, arranging my full costume, someone going grouse shooting on the moors. I could feel Miss P's puzzlement and annoyance like radar through the wall. My hair looked the way it always does when it's wet. I was going to have metal snaps attached to my skull so the beret would stay on in a blizzard.

Denise was there at the end of the row of lockers, looking at me with something close to suspicion, her bathing cap dangling off a finger.

"That's great," she said, meaning it, but also going out of her way to *sound* like she meant it, so she didn't—it sounded forced.

She eyed my lady-of-the-manor garb and gave her swimsuit a tug at the butt, maybe a habit she picked up from me. One trouble with swimsuits: when you talk to someone dressed like a clothes store you feel at a disadvantage.

Denise came toward me with an air of caution, and sat. She

toyed with a terry-cloth towel, flicking it and rolling it. Her toe-nails dilapidated, ragged quarter moons. She hunched on the bench and splashed her toes in a tiny puddle, like maybe I had forgotten she was there.

It's amazing how little insight some people have, how little sense of what others feel.

I unzipped the backpack and slipped the envelope from its pocket. I smoothed the gentle wrinkles with my fingers. In my fantasy I had kept reconstructing what would happen next. I would slip it under Miss P's office door. I would leave it on her desk, on top of a pile of fitness equipment catalogs. Or maybe I would hand it to her in person.

A dozen people slamming into a locker room can be deafening. "Way to go," said one voice after another. "Looking good, Bonnie," the dumb, earnest things people say to one another.

Lockers open with a bang almost as loud as when they slam shut, the force of voices and laughter resounding in the metal compartments around us.

Charlotte Witt, the full-bodied star of the Sacramento Invitational, stopped me outside Miss P's office and said she was so happy I was myself again. Charlotte Witt has the classy air of an extremely athletic First Lady, the sort of person who sounds phony saying good morning. Miss P had taken her time entering the fog and noise of the locker room, but I felt her consciousness groping toward mine, puzzled that I had not come back to talk to her, wondering what was on my mind.

The envelope contained my letter to Ms. Petrossian, resigning from the team. The message covered three lines, telling her that it was time for me to put my diving career behind me. I surprised myself—I carried the envelope outside, like someone looking for a mailbox, then zipped it into my pack.

I carried it home, and slipped it into the bottom drawer of my dresser.

CHAPTER

TWENTY-SIX

Every morning I rose in the darkness and did my running—"roadwork," Dad always called it. I reached a new level of stamina, up-slope, down-slope, all the same to me.

I worked out at the academy pool from noon until late every afternoon. Miss P gave me her standard encouragement, even making a joke of it, telling me to jog it when I was limping with exhaustion, then laughing, showing she was just kidding. She had little to say to me aside from coach chatter. Maybe she saw something independent in my comeback, something that had nothing to do with her.

Only once did she stop me at poolside, swinging her brass whistle on a string. "Don't forget to breathe," she said. "Long in, long out." She waited for me to acknowledge her words, like someone transmitting on shortwave.

I studied fresh videos of my dives every evening. Rowan watched with me, when he wasn't in Carmel or Stinson Beach.

I freeze-framed the image of myself as I powered upward, as I tumbled, as I knifed into the water.

"I look terrible," I would say. "Like a mannequin. Bonnie, the diving robot." I'd push fast forward, through the jerky, streaking figures of other divers, until it was me again. Every diver I would face at Stanford would be much better than I was. Sometimes after I turned off the TV I was too depressed to talk.

My mother watched with us if she got home in time, and while Rowan exclaimed, "Another great one, Bonnie!" I just sat there and stared at the screen. You could see the fear in my knees, in my shoulders, my face.

In California a preliminary hearing is held within a week or two of the arraignment. It's a miniature trial, with witnesses and cross examination, a chance for the People and the Accused to probe the strengths of the upcoming case. My father's preliminary was set for the beginning of the following week, and as the day approached I felt the chill seep further into my bones. I wished there was some way the hearing could be postponed, or set aside indefinitely, lost in dog-eared files of paperwork.

That weekend Jack Stoughton was on his way to a Save the Presidio fund-raiser in San Francisco. He was motoring across Van Ness Avenue when a driver ran a red light. The footage on Channel Two ten o'clock news showed a sad mess of Jaguar, and the unmistakable profile of Jack chatting with the paramedics as they loaded him into the ambulance. The paramedics were smiling, and one of them, a woman, laughed, her head thrown back, evidently entirely unaware of the camera.

The KNBR reporter on the scene deplored the rash of hit-and-run accidents. Jack was interviewed in the hospital, with his head perched on top of a neck brace that made his spine look absurdly long, like a llama's. "I had no idea what hit me," said Jack, in a tone of merriment. The tape was edited at that point—you could see the jump cut.

"Pain killers," said Mom from her place in the shifting shadows of the living room. Her laptop was beside her, throwing a bluish light into her eyes. "Hear how he slurred?" Her white bird-of-paradise was in the advance edition of the Sunday paper, looking like a blossom from a distant galaxy.

Cindy called Sunday night. The preliminary hearing would be postponed, and she and Dad were off to Bourbon Street.

"You couldn't buy such luck," Mom said.

Mom took me out on my birthday, to a place called Shark's, overlooking the marina, red and yellow lights on the water. The staff sang "Happy Birthday" in harmony, the rum-chocolate cake crowded, seventeen pink candles. She gave me one of those ugly/pretty Hermes scarves and a gold Cross pen. Georgia had sent me a copy of *Taber's Cyclopedic Medical Dictionary*, and I got a couple dozen cards from people I knew and liked, athletes, distant aunts. My father was always late with his card and a check, so I hadn't expected anything.

"This was so long overdue," said Mrs. Beal.

"We should have done this an age ago," said her husband.

Rowan winked at me. A servant—what else could I call her?—looked in from the doorway to see if I had spilled any of my peas. It was the day after my birthday, and the Beals were all having wine, jewel-glass goblets of ruby fluid poured from one of those bottles that give you lead poisoning from the cork seal. I had asked for ice water. They all toasted me, wishing me many happy returns.

It was the first time I had ever eaten dinner with the Beals, and I had the impression I was under careful scrutiny. The *Tribune* had run two articles about my father, and KTVU had featured Jack Stoughton in a smaller, less-padded neck brace, saying that his client would be "absolutely exonerated." In the aftermath of this wash of news about my father, I sensed that everyone studied me from afar.

Even the Beals' invitation had to be viewed as a kind of test, an oral exam, whether or not I was up to their standards. I had come to recognize that there was a snappish, impatient side to Rowan's father. But tonight Mr. Beal gazed across the table with the kindly, energetic manner of the vicar who poisons half his parishioners.

"Rowan says you're back to full form, diving," he offered. This was an odd way of putting it, and I wondered if he had said *full form*, and then realized that it might refer to my figure, not my customary level of skill. So he added "diving," to avoid embarrassing himself.

"She's better than ever," said Rowan. "We can still buy tickets for the Pacific Invitational."

"We should," murmured his father, in the tone of someone who had no serious intention of following through.

Maybe they were observing my table manners, how I managed to eat the dainty, half-raw lamb chop. "I am nowhere near what I need to be," I said, knife and fork perfectly obedient to my hand. The ice cubes in the water were those round shouldered ingots you see in ads for scotch. I wondered if the servant, a gray-haired woman with the steady eye of a dental hygienist, got up first thing in the morning to chisel the cubes.

Mrs. Beal was dazzling in a blue sweater and a loop of pearls, the yellow-tinted variety. "How is your mother doing, through all this?" she asked, either forgetting that my parents were divorced or exhibiting such sterling good manners that a little detail like divorce made no difference.

I was ready. "We are distressed at how the justice system is being misused," I said. "My sister Georgia is coming down to be at the preliminary. The assistant DA, Montie Carver, the one with the blond hair down to here, is the kind of hired gun who takes one look at a community activist like my dad—" And aches to shoot him down, I was about to say, but stopped myself. Was there a delicate way to express these impressions?

"He's a hungry prosecutor," said Mr. Beal, in the same way he would have said *hungry weasel.* "One of the best."

I had been pretending to know more than I did. I had seen Carver's name in headlines in the *Chronicle*, and I had glimpsed his face on Eyewitness News. I knew he had a reputation as an aggressive attorney in cases involving fraud against senior citizens, but I had taken hope at the fact that he was an *assistant* district attorney. Glancing down at my saffron rice, I felt uneasy.

"But Bonnie's father has Jack Stoughton in his camp," said Rowan breezily.

"Oh, well, in that case," said Mr. Beal, with just a little too much haste, "we can look forward to a happy resolution."

"Key lime pie for dessert," Mrs. Beal whispered, bending close.

Georgia arrived late the night before the preliminary hearing. I was telling myself I wasn't apprehensive about the next day, but the knock at the door nearly stopped my heart.

I hurried to open it. A woman who looked very much like Mom gave me a grin, the porch light gilding her features. I hadn't remembered her being quite so tall or heavyset.

"I'm sorry I'm late," she said. "I dropped by to see Dad."

This shouldn't have surprised me, but I was suddenly full of questions about what she thought about Cindy's taste in art, Dad's improvements to his back garden. And how Dad looked to her.

But you don't hurry Georgia. She told us all about her new pickup, a Ford Ranger. "It's amazing how they gear trucks so low," she said, mystifying me. "You go ten miles an hour, you have to shift out of first." She was wearing a denim skirt and old-fashioned tennis shoes, the canvas kind you can throw into the washing machine. Her top was a plaid lumberjack flannel, Northwoods chic.

Mom made us melted cheese sandwiches, an old family favorite, although Georgia gave me a conspiratorial purse of the
lips when Mom wasn't looking: Who eats these things any
more?

She ate every crumb. It was wonderful to have her there. She
gave her husband a call, saying she had arrived safely. I
couldn't help overhearing. She called him *Sweetie*. She was always reminding him to take vitamin E or wear a warmer
sweater. Paul was finishing a degree in highway engineering.
He worked as a dispatcher for Cal Trans, telling road crews
where to find broken branches and washed-out pavement on
Highway One.

"Brilliant!" said Georgia, congratulating Myrna on her litter.
The cat leaned into Georgia's legs, purring. Sometimes you
think cats must have excellent memories, instant recall of their
friends.

It was good to see Georgia, but it also underscored the crisis
we were in. It was the sort of overly cheerful mood I associated
with my grandparents' funerals, everyone chattering, afraid to
shut up. My sister asked me how my brain was functioning,
"after they stuffed it back inside your head."

I let it stay jokey, how it turned out the human brain wasn't
all that important.

Georgia told us things we already knew, that she was studying manipulatives for children, how play can be the same as
learning. She was studying at Humboldt State, learning how to

organize activity areas with good sightlines. She said it was definite, she was going to be a kindergarten teacher.

"I'm so glad!" said Mom, in a tone of such feeling, I had to realize once again that Mom wished I had more ordinary goals, swimming instead of diving.

Then, in a low, intent tone, Mom asked, "What did you think of Cindy?"

Georgia gave a little nonlaugh, one of Mom's.

"Really?" Mom said.

Georgia made no sound.

My mother said, "That's what I was afraid of."

I had hoped Georgia and I would talk long into the night. I had even set aside my most recent video, but Georgia said that driving always tired her out, and she would be worthless tomorrow if she didn't get some sleep.

It was the sort of thing Mom said, that she would be worthless if she didn't eat soon, or rest for a while. Besides, there was a silence about Georgia, things she didn't want to say. When I went to bed, I tried to sense my sister's presence in the house. Was that her, running water in the back bathroom, closing the closet door in her old bedroom?

Maybe I was hoping she would scratch at my door and sneak in, like in the old days, so she could tell me about a book she was reading, a poltergeist in a South Dakota farmhouse, or a region in the Caribbean Sea cruise ships sailed across never to be heard from again.

Before the divorce Dad sometimes read us stories. Georgia came into my bedroom, older, allowed to stay up an hour later. One of our favorite tales was about a rabbit who dressed up in bark and branches to scare the daylights out of a fox. My father imitated the rabbit in a deep, chilling voice: "I am the spirits of all the rabbits you have eaten, Brother Fox!"

A blind pedestrian would have little trouble crossing streets in downtown Oakland. Traveling roughly west to east, when the signal changes to green, an electronic *twirp twirp* sounds. The signal to cross north to south is the call of a cuckoo. Georgia and I parked her pickup in a pay lot on Alice Street, and passed one of the white Alameda County Sheriff's buses, a new load of prisoners facing justice. Mom had explained how busy she was, so my sister and I marched up the steps to the courthouse, just the two of us, Georgia keeping up matter-of-fact chatter, lumber mills closing, her septic tank backing up.

The first sign you see is WARNING WEAPONS PROHIBITED. Georgia took one look at this and said, "Damn!" And I couldn't keep from laughing.

CHAPTER

TWENTY-EIGHT

The prosecutor, Montie Carver, had one of those tans you know come from a tanning booth, every inch of his body under his clothes the same unblemished bronze. His yellow hair was expensively long, and except for his gray suit and cuff links he looked like the kind of parking lot attendant who collected big tips.

My father wore one of the suits he had hand tailored in a shop off Union Square. It was a suit that didn't look expensive, the sort of business outfit you barely notice, with a crisp white shirt and a dark tie. When he saw Georgia and me he gave us a thumbs-up, and he nodded and gave his award-winning smile to acquaintances in the courthouse audience.

But the courtroom was crowded, and many of the people saw my father's smile and looked right back, unsmiling, stonily silent. Cindy occupied a seat in the front row, a navy blue, nearly nautical blouse, her hair gathered back into a gold clasp. The effect was prim; she looked younger than I did.

The witness swore to tell the truth and took his seat. Carver asked him to state his name and occupation. He was Allen Post, the owner of a foundry that manufactured every kind of manhole cover, from the big steel disks you see in intersections to the little ones in the sidewalk that seal pipes and cables. "People walk on my product all the time, and never know it," said Mr. Post.

Carver didn't bother looking at his notes, but unlike the lawyers you see in movies, he didn't wander around the courtroom. "Mr. Post, did you file a suit with the Isabella Construction Company?"

"Yes, my new house—the house I had built—was a delight to my wife and myself. It was a beautiful place, but it had cracks in its foundation."

Carver raised a hand, glanced at Her Honor, and cautioned the witness not to answer everything all at once, let the testimony come out little by little. The judge was a woman with white hair and glasses, the theatrical sort of glasses frames that make the person wearing them look small and big-eyed.

"Who was your legal representative during this lawsuit?" asked Carver.

Mr. Post had a gray mustache and shaggy gray hair surrounding a bald spot. A broad shouldered, ham-fisted man, he looked like he could pick up a manhole cover and skim it like a Frisbee. He could not help looking briefly at my father as he answered, "Harvey Chamberlain."

"Was your lawsuit successful, Mr. Post?"

"There were cracks you could put your hand into, and this is a three-story house, with a view of the whole Bay Area. A view like a jewel box. But the first serious rain and the structure was going to slide."

"Mr. Post," said Carver, with a little laugh. "Could you answer my question?"

"The construction company settled out of court," said Mr. Post.

"What was the amount of the settlement?"

"The entire house had to be jacked off its mooring, the old foundation broken up. It was our dream house, my wife and I planned that place our whole lives."

"If you could tell us the amount of the settlement, Mr. Post."

"Five hundred thousand dollars."

"When did you receive this payment from the construction company?"

Mr. Post found it difficult to say: "I never did."

"Did you ever receive any explanation for this?"

"A zillion explanations." The witness did not want to look at anyone, gripping the wooden arms of the chair. "Every time I called Mr. Chamberlain, he said the company still hadn't sent the check. For two years, he said the construction company was sitting on the money."

Jack sat beside my father, his head in a medical turtleneck. With every question my father's attorney seemed to grow a little taller in the chair.

"What did you do?" asked Carver.

"After so much time, I couldn't wait any longer. I got on the phone myself, made some calls, to the president of the construction company. He said they had sent a check to my lawyer, Mr. Chamberlain, for the entire amount, right after the settlement had been reached."

Jack hitched himself to his feet, objecting.

Georgia craned her neck as Mrs. Jovanovich found her way to the witness stand. "It's dear old Mrs. What's-her-name," whispered Georgia in a tone of surprise.

It took a long time for her to cross the courtroom with the help of two metal canes tipped with white rubber. Finally, a bailiff, with his holster and his badge, offered her an arm, and she made it to the witness stand at last.

She is the kind of woman you imagine as an empress, elderly but in full command of both her army and her navy. When she speaks, though, you are reminded of the inroads age has made on her powers.

"And what legal help did you seek in managing your estate, Mrs. Jovanovich?" Carver was asking.

"I couldn't begin to collect the rents and deal with the tax documents, and then when one of my properties had fire damage, and an apartment building suffered in one of our earthquakes, I had so many pieces of paper it was bewildering."

Carver met the judge's eyes. "Just take your time, Mrs. Jovanovich, " he said, gently, but speaking clearly, "and answer the questions slowly. We all want to hear what you have to say."

"And please speak right into the microphone," said the judge with the sort of kindly smile people give frail people.

Mrs. Jovanovich crooked the mike a little closer, with something like a practiced touch, and her voice resounded. "I asked Harvey Chamberlain to help me, and he said he would."

"He acted as your attorney?"

"He was my legal and financial advisor. In collecting insurance money, pursuing money owed to me, and in helping sort though my expenses. I have so much to do, and I can't do it all anymore, Mr. Carver. Mr. Chamberlain is always such a pleasure to be with. He is so full of life. My late husband and he used to play golf together, although I do believe Mr. Chamberlain let my husband win."

Carver slumped a little. "Could you estimate for us, Mrs. Jovanovich, the size of your estate, in terms of dollars?"

"I should have brought my financial records with me," said Mrs. Jovanovich. "I'm so terribly sorry—"

"Just roughly, to the best of your recollection," said Carver.

"Oh, I'm afraid I deal with hundreds of thousands of dollars, Mr. Carver. I have to apologize, because I know some people have so little." Her face wrinkled into a kindly apology, as though ashamed of her relative wealth. "My husband and I worked hard to build up a considerable amount of property."

"Could you tell us, please, how you began to question the professional services Mr. Chamberlain was providing?"

"You phrase it so politely, Mr. Carver," said Mrs. Jovanovich.

"You're being very kind, and I appreciate it." She lifted a finger to silence Carver, and continued, "I discovered that Mr. Chamberlain was deceiving me. He was robbing me."

Jack climbed to his feet, said something in an exasperated tone, but before the judge could address the witness, Mrs. Jovanovich's amplified voice was saying, "Mr. Chamberlain is a thief."

CHAPTER

TWENTY-NINE

Whenever the microphone shifted away from her voice, Mrs. Jovanovich gripped it and got it right back where everyone could hear what she was saying. Dad sat with his hands folded at his lips, making a tent of his forefingers. I couldn't see his eyes, but I knew he was gazing upward at the blank wall above the judge.

Georgia folded her arms, one of my mother's postures. The courtroom began to get warm. I closed my eyes, and when I opened them, the colors were even more vivid than before, the egg-yellow collar of the man sitting in front of me, the glittering cuff link on Carver's sleeve. I wondered if I could slip past the spectators, to the door, and out into the corridor.

Sometimes when I closed my eyes the floor of the courtroom seemed to yaw beneath me, swing down and away, and I was falling. I gripped the edge of my chair. I reminded myself I was fine, right beside Georgia. Sometimes the judge slipped off her glasses, and her eyes looked small and vulnerable, a pink dint on either side of her nose.

The judge announced a two-hour recess for lunch, and Georgia and I tried to swim toward Dad, upstream against the flow of spectators. Dad put his arm around Cindy, caught my eye and gave a little shake of his head, like a boxer making light of a hard punch: Not even close.

I gave him a brave lift of my chin, unable to force through the crowd. "Later," mouthed Dad.

He turned to Jack and the two of them looked wrapped in lawyer/client privilege, Dad nodding as Jack confided to him. I got close enough to hear, "Vietnamese on Jackson, or we could go for the veggie burgers across the street from the Paramount—"

"Just so long as there isn't any garlic," said Cindy. Dad kept a grip on her arm, like she was about to faint, or escape.

Jack saw me and gave a wave of his hand, like a man clearing away gnats, the charges against my father so many tiny bugs. Jack's cross-examination had consisted of prompting Mrs. Jovanovich to admit that my father had provided a nurse, employed a tax accountant, and fired a gardener who passed out under the Chinese elm. Mrs. Jovanovich's attitude had been one of genteel correction: Yes, Mr. Chamberlain had helped, for a fee, but he had also opened the mail, forged her signature, and, allowing herself a touch of slang, he had "maxed out my credit cards."

Georgia and I didn't talk for a while, but Georgia has an ability to make you feel included in whatever she is doing without actually using the power of speech.

She paused meaningfully outside a door marked MEN, and continued her search. Everywhere we looked on the fourth floor we saw corridors full of videocams and smartly dressed men and women talking into tape recorders. My sister and I were both dressed like secretarial students, dark skirts, unsexy white blouses, mine with demure pinstripes. My sister was at the point she might consider losing a few pounds when she got back to Eureka, or at least try a more slimming exercise than chopping cordwood.

The women's room was nearly empty. I looked wan, my eyes like two holes, and I considered wearing the beret over my face. Georgia said she wasn't very hungry, her first actual English sentence in quite some time. We shared a stick of Doublemint. But we couldn't stay in the lavatory forever. A husky sheriff's department deputy leaned into her image at the mirror, working a cold sore with her tongue.

The courthouse has narrow hallways for such a big building, and floors the color of goose-liver paté. We passed by an espresso/cappuccino stand in the lobby and stood outside, blinking in the sunlight, saying it was really stupid to forget sunglasses on a day like this.

Downtown Oakland is a landscape of Kinko's copiers and One-Hour Martinizing, interspersed with hotel lobbies, cool, dark interiors exhaling decades of cigarette funk. Georgia and I avoided the potholes and the neat stacks of pallets in the warehouse district.

At last the masts of the Marina gleamed. A Coast Guard cutter purred slowly outward, toward the open bay. We strolled along the gangway, sailboats and motor yachts nuzzling their moorings, and I felt hope begin again, the salt air and the sun having a cheering effect on both of us.

The *Queen Athena* was not in her berth. The gray-green bilge of the marina lifted and slowly fell as the wake of the Coast Guard vessel reached this far. Georgia and I leaned on the rail and gazed into the empty mooring.

I tried to imagine Jack and Dad racing here, plunging onto the deck, starting up the *Queen*'s engines, and powering her out to the open harbor, a nautical lunch break. But the lazy, gently disturbed surface of the water made this unlikely. No boat had stirred this water in hours.

"Dad's selling the boat," said Georgia, squinting in the reflected sunlight.

"He told you that?" I asked, startled.

"No." The wind was rising, a rope rhythmically slapping a mast. A flag fluttered in the distance, a dove-tailed yacht club pennant. "He wouldn't let me in on anything," my sister said.

Georgia was quiet, shielding her face from the light with her hand. Then she said, "Did he tell you he was innocent?"

I didn't like the way she asked.

We ordered spring rolls, and the waiter brought out a small haystack of bean sprout appetizer, bowls of rice, and a pot of tea too hot to touch. The chopsticks slipped from their paper sleeve, wooden utensils stuck together. You tug them apart, but the break is never clean, and I worried at the tear with my fingernail, smoothing a splinter. The green tea was still too hot. There was a flock of customers eager to pay at the cash register.

"He's liquidating everything," she said. "Putting his money into objects he can sell fast when he has to."

"You don't know this."

Georgia agreed. She didn't really *know* anything. "Dad wouldn't talk to me seriously. He just said everything would work out, and got me talking about the classes I'm taking in the fall. Cindy did some talking when I helped her load the dishwasher. She said whatever a person did, she had to plan ahead. She also said the time in New Orleans wasn't anything like the break they needed, she'd love to see Seattle, Aspen, Key West."

"Jack's expensive," I suggested, still unsteady at the thought of Dad without his boat.

For a while there was no further conversation. The spring rolls arrived, tubes of crisp batter and vegetables. For an instant a thought electrified me: Dad would escape, with a briefcase full of currency, to Ixtapa, Belize, Tonga.

"He married Cindy so they could take advantage of spousal privilege," Georgia said. "After all, she *was* his secretary. She can't be forced to testify against him." Her voice was soft, her hands cradling a cup of tea.

"You're making this up."

Georgia said, "He'll never practice law again."

It didn't sound like me, a harsh voice. "Who's been lying to you, Georgia?"

She took her time before she said anything more. "Last night before I went to sleep, I knocked at Mother's door."

She hesitated, giving me time to say I didn't want to hear this.

"I asked her what she knew," she continued. "And she said, 'Ask your father. Ask him what happens to an attorney who rips off his clients. Ask why the partnership broke up, why Adam David refused to share an office with your father anymore.'"

The restaurant was nearly empty now, dishes clattering in the kitchen, a place of sudden crowd, sudden quiet.

"As though I could ever talk to Dad," said Georgia, "about anything."

I put my elbows on the table. *Long in,* I reminded myself, *long out.*

"Don't be angry with Mother," said Georgia. When, I wondered, had she stopped calling her Mom?

I wasn't going to say anything until I was ready.

Georgia tasted the tea. "You're the only person who can ask him to tell the truth."

My emotions were under control now. I spoke emphatically, spacing out the words. "I cannot believe I am hearing this."

I considered several ways to express my next thought, like someone translating from a foreign language. "You know what word occurs to me right now?" I asked. I sounded a little like Dad.

"What word?" asked Georgia at last, in a small, weary voice.

I got up and left her there, barreled out into the sunlight and kept walking.

I didn't return to the courthouse that afternoon. I suited up and did my dives in the academy pool. After an hour of somersaults I was hanging onto the side of the pool, breathing hard. Miss P asked me how I was doing.

Betrayal.

I swam laps for a long time that afternoon. I freestyled until I could barely move my arms and legs. Even then I didn't want to leave the water. I sat dangling my feet in the water, while the pool gradually stopped quaking and reflected the windows above.

CHAPTER

THIRTY

When I got home Georgia was sitting in the front seat of her Ford Ranger, the engine running. I asked her how the afternoon at the courthouse had gone, and she said that Cindy sucked white-and-green peppermints all afternoon. "She put the cellophane wrappers in her purse," Georgia said.

I was late, Mom and Georgia finished with good-byes, Mom on the porch, the farewell ceremonies over, except for me. The streetlights were on, and the neighboring houses hummed with evening, television, quiet voices, a sprinkler on down the street, glittering drops of water.

"It's okay," Georgia said, meaning it was all right, me leaving the restaurant.

I wonder how many important conversations my family has had, an engine running, someone ready to head for the freeway.

"I shouldn't have done that," I said, my voice so soft she might not have heard me.

She gave a tilt of her head, quick acknowledgment. "They

didn't set a court date," Georgia said. "But the judge said there was sufficient case to warrant a trial."

I hadn't wanted to come out and ask.

I couldn't forgive Georgia for her feelings about our father. I could only remind myself that she was married to a guy who loved the elasticity of concrete and was always picking up a virus, nasal infections, earaches. I used to hope Georgia would be a journalist or a world traveler, a woman with a briefcase. "Jack should have torn those witnesses to pieces," I said.

She left a space in the conversation, where she would have said what she thought about Jack, and about the case against Dad. She wished me luck with Miss P. That's how she put it, not wanting to say *Good luck with the diving*, knowing how athletes feel about saying certain things, how words can cause misfortune.

She patted my hand, having to reach out of the car and wave her hand in the air for a moment before I realized what she wanted. I held out my own arm, and she touched me, gave me a squeeze. Then she was gone, waving up and down, like someone flying with one hand, until I could not see her car any more.

I didn't even have time to tell her, "Say hi to Sweetie."

A couple of days later I dropped by Dad's house and ran into LaTanya, the temp from Dad's office, picking up the mail and putting a fat, pale rubber band around the throwaway ads. "Mr. Chamberlain's taking a vacation," said LaTanya with a sympathetic, regal air, car keys tinkling.

I bicycled past the house when I had a chance, and jogged by each dawn.

The lamps in my father's living room ran on a timer, so the front drapes lit up faithfully at seven-thirty and glowed until dawn. I made the place the destination of my morning miles. I stood breathing hard, flexing my legs, stalling. Hoping the lights would come on again, a silhouette on its way to make coffee.

"I used to worry, the way you do now," my mother said, up to her elbows in planting mulch. "Where he was, who he was with. Where the money was coming from." The tropical peat was rich, clinging, like coffee grounds. She prodded the lop-sided Y of a ti plant root into the mulch. "Until one day I realized he was going to take me down with him."

I kept quiet, sprinkling a few scattered crumbs of soil into the pot. I couldn't help recalling what she had said when I told her Dad had been arrested. *You need to think about you.*

I wonder if Mom had given her own past some thought, her own secrets. "Maybe I still feel a sort of loyalty," she continued. "Maybe I looked the other way so long I can't say anything, if I wanted to. I'm not the one who can answer your questions."

I almost said, I don't have any questions.

CHAPTER

THIRTY-ONE

Rowan ran with me that morning, huffing along, more and more out of breath.

I ran backward, in no hurry, calling encouragement while he dodged the red plastic space guns and tricycles, the toys kids leave on the sidewalk. "Go on," he would gasp, and when I jackrabbited ahead I could hear him far down the street, breathing hard.

Rowan wasn't in such bad shape. It was me—I had never been in better condition. I ran easily up Dad's street, the morning sun in my eyes, and when I saw him I couldn't be sure who it was.

I *was* sure, but I didn't want to be disappointed. The sun behind him was so strong it seemed to cut him in two, a bleary image I squinted to make out.

"Champion!"

I stopped in the middle of the street, hands on my hips.

He was wearing baggy shorts and a silk shirt with hibiscus

blossoms, a man on permanent vacation. I walked up the lawn and he gave me a hug, although I was embarrassed because I was a little sweaty, a spot or two of perspiration soaking through my academy T-shirt.

He turned back to unlock the car in the driveway, a low-slung, exotic-looking automobile. Rowan jogged up the driveway, and Dad asked how it was going, the way men do, so casual and macho they are inarticulate.

"New car?" I heard myself ask.

"Jack loaned me one of his," he said. He swung the door open and I had a glimpse of a leather interior, the seats worn dark. "An old XKE—it needs all kinds of repairs."

"That was nice of him," I said. Niceness was a concept I had picked up from Mom. Calling an act of generosity *good* made it sound heavy-handed.

"That depends how you look at it," said Dad.

"Decent body work, though," said Rowan.

"Jack's part owner of a shop down in Monterey," said Dad. "Specializes in detailing." He slammed the door and fussed with his key chain. The key made a quiet click, and Dad gave us a lift of his eyebrows, letting us in on the question: Will it start?

The engine chattered and stalled. "Every time I turn the key, it's major malfunction," said Dad. "This is one of those cars so beautiful it's about to fall apart."

He was tanned and had lost weight. Neighbors would be watching, a curtain parting, slipping shut.

"We'll set up some tennis," he said. "I bet Rowan's got a killer serve." The car coughed and fell silent again. The car rolled a short distance down the driveway, grit crackling under the tires.

I asked, "Where were you?"

For a moment it was like he hadn't heard me. He set the parking brake, fumbled with a knob on the dash. "Cindy had never seen Tahoe, can you believe that? We rented a cabin with a view of the lake, and a power boat, one of those Formula 27 PCs. I bought a couple of wet suits, some water skis."

"You had a good time?"

"The best," he said.

"Maybe it has a manual choke," said Rowan, leaning on the car.

"It's flooded," said Dad.

A moment passed, my dad fidgeting with the gearshift. "You're not worried, are you, Champ?" he asked gently. "I'm going to come from behind, just like Silky Sullivan. You know the story of Silky Sullivan?" Dad was saying, talking to Rowan, about to embark on a story I had heard a hundred times.

Rowan grinned, a perfect audience, chuckling at all the right places in the tale.

Dad fell silent at last.

"That's great," said Rowan, unaware that he had heard a third-rate version of the story.

Dad started the car, the air heavy with the scent of carbon and sulfur. "Jack had the smog device disconnected," said Dad with a grin: Hope I don't get caught.

He backed out of the driveway and floored the accelerator, the Jaguar roaring slowly up the street.

Cindy called just before school started in September. "I don't have time to talk right now," she said. "I just thought you ought to know."

I was in a hurry myself, getting ready to see a play at Berkeley Rep with Mom, hopping on one foot, pulling on a pair of what Mom called "sensible shoes."

I sat on the edge of the bed. "What's wrong?"

"I want you to hear it from me first," she said. What she meant was: You were the one I knew I could talk to. Then she took a moment, like I was supposed to guess.

When I didn't she said, "Harvey's going to plead."

THIRTY-TWO

Myrna's six kittens were all dark and long haired, and looked like very furry hamsters. Gradually they turned into cats—acrobats, climbing the living room drapes, boxing the grape ivy, thundering up and down stairs. I sat and watched them, calling them the way my family does, that little noise with my tongue. Still, it was obvious that Myrna would never lose her obsession with her litter. She would remain a single-minded, frantically devoted mother forever, huge cats hanging onto her nipples.

All Mom had to do was flash a few Polaroids at her customers, and when someone said, "What darling kittens!" it was easy to find new homes. We kept one, a gray-blue male Mom called Bucket. When all the other kittens were gone, Myrna didn't notice. Maybe she couldn't count.

Mom attended the sentencing, dressed in a somber wool skirt and jacket she rarely wore. She sat with Georgia and me at the back of the courtroom. We had never discussed whether or not she would come along. When the morning came, she said that she would drive us, and it was plain that she intended to sit there, too, whatever happened. I was wearing a new navy-blue skirt and a white blouse, no jacket; I looked like a stewardess on a hot day.

Dad wore a suit, a new gray three-piece. Cindy wore a sherbet outfit thing, with a yellow scarf, and a costume jewelry insect on her breast, like someone auditioning for hostess at a pancake restaurant. I almost said something to Georgia about what awful clothes, but Cindy had drawn on her lipstick badly, one point of her upper lip higher than the other, and sat straight up in her chair, no one to either side of her.

Montie Carver and Jack spoke before the judge arrived, quiet, heads together, nodding. Jack had grown a mustache, and it made him look heavier, years older. Montie had a tiny Band-Aid on the bridge of his nose.

When the judge arrived we all stood. She had a new pair of glasses, glittering gold frames.

I heard what was said, but the words sounded unreal to me. The sounds of shoes squeaking on the polished tile floor and the tiny whirring of the computers were much more loud and clear than the lumbering sounds of human speech.

When the judge read the sentencing agreement, people in the audience turned to each other with satisfied expressions, and a couple of people clapped.

I didn't expect what happened next and would have fled the

room, except I couldn't rise from my chair, and I had to sit there, unable to make a move.

Even afterward, in the fish restaurant in Berkeley, I was numb and caught up by tiny details, the salt on the crackers, the purple cabbage in the coleslaw. The restaurant had a view of San Francisco Bay. I felt it was wrong to be here, as if we were celebrating, even though I know that mourners often treat themselves to decent food; life is hard enough, they might as well enjoy the chowder.

Georgia and my mother made conversation about a stilt or a shearwater, some sort of bird, hunting lunch at the edge of the bay. Georgia liked wildlife, but Mom rarely commented on the behavior of nature. This particular waterfowl got a lot of comment, dodging persistently among the lapping waves far below the restaurant. "I'm not one of those people who would like to be a bird," Mom said.

"Paul said to send his best," said Georgia as the plates arrived, as though the commencement of serious eating was somehow ceremonial. The waitress got us all set, tartar sauce in little paper cups, and then Mom and Georgia picked up their forks.

If I had said anything at all, I would have said how surprised I was. I had not expected the handcuffs—the way he walked hunched beside the bailiff, suit jacket buckled outward from his chest.

CHAPTER

THIRTY-THREE

I laced my shoes and tiptoed my way through the dark rooms of the house.

I didn't have to be so quiet that morning—Mom was doing her laps. She had begun getting up early, expanding her business to include cut flowers, dried ornamentals. She had arranged the flowers for a wedding in Tilden Park, white wicker flower stands anchored with bricks inside, where no one could see. I watched her swim, feeling strangely protective, someone who could pull her from the water if there was an emergency.

I couldn't help reading one of her memos on the dining room table, her reply to someone's e-mail, telling him she didn't want any scrawny Halfmoon-Bay roses, she'd pay air freight from Nipomo.

It was a week after the sentencing. I stretched a little on the dewy lawn, grass clippings sticking to the sides of my shoes. I headed uphill, pushing myself hard.

I maneuvered back over the Warren Freeway and found myself getting a little warm and a little sweaty by the time I was almost all the way to the Beals' house. I sat at their curb. Mrs. Beal was perfectly nice on the phone, but you could *hear* her being perfect, a touch of effort in her voice. The family was keeping Rowan busy, taking him to play tennis with a state senator's daughter, but he called me often, even when he was out of town.

I searched along the curb, up the sidewalk, stooping, discarding. The early sun made so many things sparkle—not all of them were pretty when you took them in your hand.

I put a white pebble inside their mailbox, a fragment of quartz. It was something to mention when I spoke to him on the phone: *By the way, did you get my rock?*

When I had showered and was in my street outfit, denim pants and a tropical blue cashmere sweater Mom gave me when one of her clients paid her a bonus, I stood at the top of the stairs.

Mom was in the back garden, out by the fishpond, on the phone, from the sound of it. I think I caught the word "azaleas," Mom planning an order for the winter, months away. Pink azaleas. She never used to bother with shrubs like that. From the top of the stairs, I could see a heap of papers, catalogs, invoices, not far from where Myrna was asleep, her tail and one white leg just within view.

I hesitated.

Quietly, soundlessly, I slipped into Mom's bedroom. I opened the closet door.

I stood still, listening. She was still outside, a vague voice from so far away she was almost inaudible.

I stooped, nudging the closet door to one side, the shoe organizer stuffed full of custom-made sandals and patent-leather pumps Mom always said she was too tall to wear. The three steel boxes were still there.

But the boxes looked different from the way they had the last time I saw them, months before. They were labeled FIREPROOF, as always. But each one was unlocked, not closed all the way. I opened one of them, hinging back the lid. It was empty.

All three of them were empty.

CHAPTER

THIRTY-FOUR

I descended the stairs, taking each step deliberately. I knelt before the fireplace.

At first it looked as pristine as ever, the deluxe latex paint unmarred.

But I studied it. Someone had lit a fire here, not recently—no ash smudged my finger as I ran it along the cold iron of the grill. The ghosts of flames flickered up along the painted brick interior. Someone had cleaned out the fireplace with care, and scrubbed the cracks between the bricks.

Mom was in the kitchen, greeting one of the cats, "How are you this morning, Bucket?"

I selected a banana from the wooden bowl and peeled it. I found a plate and sliced it carefully. Some people ask why don't I eat oranges, or peaches, or mangoes.

We have North America's loudest refrigerator, a gigantic white Whirlpool that's always pumping Freon, whatever fridges do, making a noise that makes you want to yank the plug out of the wall.

I said, "Dad's protecting you."

Mom looked at me like she was surprised I was in the house.

"That's why he agreed not to fight the case," I said. "To keep you out of trouble."

Mom made one of her plosive little laughs, almost never an expression of humor.

I told her about the empty steel boxes, the signs of a fire. And I could see her considering telling me I had no business in her room, in her files. I could see her thinking, I don't have to talk. Mom could tell me that she burned up some old folders because she was sick of having them around.

I had already gone beyond what I intended to say, and I was sure she would leave the room.

"Maybe you don't want to know," she said.

I managed to send her a signal the way Georgia does, no words required.

She didn't talk right away, but there was nothing hostile or defensive about this quiet.

"Maybe I don't want to know, either," she said at last. Mom looked down at her hands, fingers spread out on the counter.

"Maybe even the divorce was a way of protecting you," I said. "Like he could see the future, a long time ago."

"That's one thing he could never see," she said.

I waited.

"But you're right. I wasn't sure. I was afraid."

When she was quiet now it was because she wanted to be fair to me—if I wanted to end this conversation, now was the time.

Mom took a few more moments before saying anything, getting my protein mix out of the cupboard, selecting a spoon. She said, "He always did things he shouldn't do. Even back then, although I never asked questions. I stayed ignorant, by choice. He helped me start my business."

"You profited from stealing," I heard myself say, unable to shut my own mouth. "The same as he did."

She didn't speak for a few heartbeats. Then she said, "I don't know for a fact that I profited from anything illegal. But I can't be certain. When I heard he was going to plead, I couldn't sleep at night. I destroyed all my old records—I didn't know what an investigator might find there. But if I profited without knowing it, Bonnie, so did you. We all did."

I went outside.

The carp in the fishpond spend their whole lives barely moving, bearded, with transparent fins, gills pumping. They are scarlet and gold, with inky black spots in places you would never expect, a tail, or a fin.

Mom joined me. She gave me a glass of protein drink, full to the brim, some of it leaking over, running onto her fingers. She washed the protein drink off her fingers in the fishpond, and the carp lifted toward her fingers, as though the stuff was something they could eat.

CHAPTER

THIRTY-FIVE

The night before the invitational I kept waking.

Audrey rustled softly in her cage, searching through the wood shavings. A mouse doesn't blink in sudden light, or squint. I turned on the desk lamp and her cinnamon-red eyes looked up into mine.

She nosed my wrist and scurried up to the crook of my arm. I was thirsty already, my heartbeat heavy.

Getting onto the bus I didn't look at anyone, I didn't talk, and no one sat near me. I sucked a lozenge to keep my mouth moist, honey-and-lemon-flavored, sugar-free.

You can see so much from a bus, pleasure boats with their graceful, pearling wakes, and tankers sitting going nowhere, waiting to deliver their oil to the Chevron refinery in Richmond. I leaned my head against the bus window, and the vibration sang into my skull. I sat upright, suddenly aware of my injury, the hair completely furred-in around the cut.

HEAT

Miss P gave each one of us a quick psych-up, telling us we were going to be great, hanging on with one hand against the movement of the bus, air brakes gasping. I could feel the cut with my fingertips.

When I imagined myself going to a university, I pictured the campus looking like Stanford, but greener. Much of Stanford is left as nature intended, which means there are tracts of brown field, oak trees in seas of golden wild rye.

I watched myself put one foot after another across the parking lot. People talked to me but I saw right through them, even Charlotte Witt, who was only apologizing for stepping on my foot. "I have to watch where I'm going," she said, bubbly with nerves.

Denise did not wear a bathing cap. She had cut all her hair off a few days before, and looked like a stranger. She wrung her hair back with her hands, a gesture she must have borrowed from me. Her dives went badly, one clumsy splash after another, and they were her usual, undramatic attempts, dives she used to own.

I think Denise missed our friendship more than I did. I couldn't help feeling a flicker of my old compassion for her—I didn't like seeing Denise fail so badly. Besides, I might pick up her bad luck.

I sat getting my breathing right the way I wanted it, hating the sight of the arena, the other divers, wanting to pay attention to nothing but my own arms and legs, the fingernails I had filed down myself.

Rowan and his father sat halfway up in the bleachers, two distinct people in a blur of strangers. Rowan stood and clapped his hands when I turned to survey the crowd, something I rarely did. You tell yourself the people out there don't matter. They do, but they almost don't. Rowan called something, but I could not make out what he was saying.

Even during the earliest heat I did not visualize my dives before I climbed the steps. I did not see them mentally from start to finish, all the way into the water. Each time I climbed from the pool I didn't bother looking toward Miss P. I didn't acknowledge the applause, if there was any. There was a space around me, a white rectangle.

At the beginning of each dive I climbed the steps, firm-footed. And it seemed I should be able to see a landscape from the top of the stairs, look out upon more than a building like an airplane hangar, a ceiling girded with black steel beams.

The judges sat at their table, with the half-distracted air of people trying to do hard math in their heads. Each time I got good altitude. My center of gravity was a pivot point in my body, a place that thrilled as I went into my tuck.

I remember wishing the pool was deeper, so the bottom would not rush toward me, my fingertips pressing, pushing it away.

Rowan and his father gave me a ride home from the academy after the bus dropped us all off. Rowan said they had been lucky to be there. This night would be one of those "gilded dates that live forever," Rowan said.

They waited in their car as I walked up the dewy front lawn of my house in the dark. I turned and waved from the front step.

I didn't open the door for a moment. I was glad to be home at last, away from the smiles and the reporters who talked their way into a ride on the bus, their little black tape recorders in hand. I thought one of them would slip in a question about my father, but no one did. They all wanted to use the word "comeback," how I had recovered from what one of them called a career-ending concussion. "And now you're one of the best prep platform specialists west of the Rockies," one had said, a man with a silver crew cut.

I let the front door swing open.

Mom could never stand to see me dive, but she always waited until late, sitting with the television picture on and the sound muted.

She wrapped her arms around me and said, "You were on the ten o'clock news."

"Okay," I said, guarded, certain that some late news had changed everything.

She said, "You were beautiful!"

The body remembers things at night. Wind, the rhythm of waves. I lay in the dark on my bed, my eyes closed, feeling the waft and rock of the water in my limbs. When I opened my eyes, I stared upward.

Only later, when I woke and sat up, did I begin to feel happy, and it was a new happiness, a little like fear. Surely the judges would change their minds. Surely by morning there would be a phone call, and it would all be taken away.

CHAPTER

THIRTY-SIX

Cindy picked me up early, when it was still dark. Only one house down the street had its lights on, a rectangle of light on the lawn. The freeway murmur on the horizon was hushed. Mom stood on the front lawn, her arms crossed. I could not see the look in her eyes, but I knew what she was thinking.

Even when it wasn't dark anymore, Cindy didn't turn off the headlights. Through the tule fog, farms glided by, barns and horses. The old Jaguar smelled of leather balm and mechanical funk, iron and oil.

Seven weeks had passed and it felt like winter. Georgia called me often, asking me how things were going. She filled me in on little details of her life, Sweetie buying her a set of watercolors, her Italian-seasoning herb garden full of thyme and not much else. I could see how someday Georgia and I might be close the way she and Mom were, no words required. We didn't talk about Dad much, but her silence was gentle.

Cindy was saying she was surprised at how many big rigs

there were, and I was agreeing that the truck traffic was bad, so early on a Saturday morning. "Don't truckers get the weekend off?" she said.

Mom had said maybe I should avoid this. Maybe it wouldn't do me any good to see him there, and besides, I didn't need the distraction. Scouts from universities had been coming to my workouts, men in sports jackets and tasseled loafers. They usually carried a video camera, but sometimes they did nothing but watch, their hands in their pockets.

The fog was so heavy Cindy had to run the windshield wipers all the way over the Altamont Pass, and as we descended into the Central Valley the visibility got worse, morning a rumor, the road ahead vague brake lights as drivers lost their nerve and slowed down.

I was tense, now that it was really happening, fussing with my new blouse, a light-weight blue rayon, tiny sleeves. I should have worn something warmer. I ran my fingers through my hair, and I could feel the tiny kiss of scar on the back of my head.

"Did you bring a roll of quarters?" Cindy asked. "Don't worry if you didn't, I still have plenty left from last time."

I had stopped by Wells Fargo Bank on MacArthur Boulevard the day before and traded in a twenty-dollar bill for two rolls. The coins felt like a handgun, weighing down my purse. But to reassure myself, I hunted for them among the Doublemint and Pilot fine-point pens. I found them, safe, right where they belonged.

"My first couple of visits I tried saying thanks, after they ran my face through the X ray twice." Her makeup kit, she meant. "Trying out a little courtesy, thinking it wouldn't hurt. They didn't exactly say, 'You're welcome.' I have come to figure politeness means nothing to someone working in a place like that."

I couldn't tell her how hard it was for me to do this. I couldn't admit to anyone the way I felt about seeing him in such a place.

"What kind of person takes that kind of job?" she was saying. Cindy did all the talking, and I urged her along. She had stories of weather, blizzards, record freezes, lightning storms so bad she was warned not to go near a telephone. "That's how you get bit," she said. "By the electricity. In the atmosphere." Her sentences short, jumpy. She chewed her Doublemint like she was trying to wear it out.

By the time we reached Modesto the sun had nearly burned through, the fence posts and even the cattle black and wet, too early in the winter for the damp to awaken the mustard or the oat weeds. I enjoyed the sight of farmhouses, like boats, single points of light.

I saw it before I knew what it was, low, flat buildings, like a factory, gray and brown, surrounded by fields just two or three weeks away from turning green.

The sign outside was surrounded by white and purple flowers, violets: SAN JOAQUIN MEN'S COLONY. Cindy searched for a place in the parking lot, the old Jaguar purring. The visitors gathered in the distance at one end of the lot, and there was nothing conspicuous about this crowd, nothing that indicated why they were here, or where they were. They could have been waiting for a Target or Walmart to open, moms and kids tired of standing up.

"We might as well make sure it's locked," said Cindy, with a wan smile, taking her time, keys, purse, double checking both doors, walking to the front of the car, checking the headlights. She let her gum drop onto the asphalt with a dainty gesture.

There were only a few men, some of them jumping up and down, hands stuffed in jeans pockets against the cold. We all waited for a gate to open in a chain-link fence, concertina barbed wire along the top. Far away through the mist a Department of Corrections officer was heading our way, blowing on his hands.

We gave my father's name, Cindy speaking with exaggerated clarity, *"Harvey Pierce Chamberlain,"* and she gave his inmate number, nine digits. This corrections officer was a red-haired woman with heavy eye makeup. She reminded me of Ms. Ashcroft, my fifth-grade teacher, who had permanent mascara tattooed around each eye. The officer located my father's name on a list and had us both sign in with the kind of pen the post office uses; your writing is half ink and half empty space.

The waiting room filled, so many children, so many women who looked my age, chewing gum, helping toddlers stand upright, gazing at the clock on the wall, five minutes to eight. At eight o'clock exactly a corrections officer began to call the names of inmates, one name at a time. The visitors would stand and arrange their clothes for a moment before they slipped through the door, a green metal barrier that closed tight for a long minute or two before the next name would be called.

The plea bargain he and Jack arranged with the DA gave him two years, eighteen months if he didn't knife anybody. Cindy said it was the easiest, and least expensive, solution. But as soon as I saw my first envelope addressed to me from the prison, I went sick. His return address was written along the lefthand edge of the envelope, not in the corner like a normal letter. And the paper was a single sheet of lined paper, not the hundred percent cotton bond he always preferred.

Cindy chewed her lip, lipstick on her front teeth. When it was our turn, we followed the corrections officer down a hallway and waited while our purses were X-rayed. Cindy had warned me to wear no jewelry. The X-ray guard handed me my purse. I thanked him, and he said, "You bet."

My heart was tripping. My letters to him were all about Rowan's video, the one he was making about otters in Monterey Bay, and about my diving, my chances at winning college scholarships.

We weren't close to seeing him, not yet. Another female guard stamped the back of my right hand, a moist kiss of ink, just above my thumb, a blurred star. I forced myself to not rub it, not try to obliterate it with spit.

Soon.

I tried to sense his presence somewhere, but there were only walls and doors, the sound of locks ratcheting, doors opening, the interior of the next room decorated with bulletin boards, a map of California, our location a circle in red ink. Our footsteps made a sound that was not quite in sync with our movements, a hushed echo.

Under the eye of a corrections officer in the shadows, we put our hands into a box of green light. The star glowed fluorescent lavender.

My mouth had a funny taste. Maybe some of the magic ink on my hand was seeping into my skin, into my nervous system. The bolt shot in another door, and we entered a very large room, the size of a good-size cafeteria. Cindy and I checked in again, an officer finding our names on a list. I printed my name in neat block letters and wrote out my signature, my entire name.

We found an empty table and two chairs. Vending machines dispensed candy along one wall, Snickers and Mars bars, bags of Fritos and barbecue-flavored potato chips. There were plastic cartons of white-bread sandwiches. I broke open one of the rolls of quarters I had brought for this very purpose and fed the machines, coming back to where Cindy was waiting. Still no sign of my father. No inmates at all yet, the room filling with visitors, children having trouble keeping their voices down.

Cindy peered into her compact, licked her teeth, and smiled like a mad woman, making sure her teeth were okay.

CHAPTER

THIRTY-SEVEN

They arrived one by one.

They each showed up at the door, took half a second to look around, and went directly to the appropriate table. What surprised me was how many of them wore glasses, the lenses gleaming in the fluorescent lights. And how many were gray-haired or bald, as though it took experience to be a prisoner here—this was not a place for beginners.

Each inmate was allowed one quick hug, a kiss, and then they had to take their seat with their hands clasped in front of them, facing the half dozen officers along one wall. The prisoners were dressed alike, a gray T-shirt and gray pants. A form letter from the Department of Corrections had warned, "no visitor will be admitted wearing gray clothing of any kind."

T-shirts always made Dad look square-shouldered and athletic. He didn't see us. Cindy stood and waved her arm side to side, a farm girl hallooing silently across a wide field. He still didn't—and then he gave a tuck of his head and a smile.

We hugged like people in an airport, joyful, but taking it in stride.

"Those sandwiches look good!" he said, prying one of the plastic cartons with his fingernail.

"I thought we'd wait for lunchtime," Cindy said, as though it was important to do things in the right order.

"Lunchtime!" he said, like he had never heard of such a silly idea.

I took a bite, tuna, with a thin patina of lettuce.

He chewed for a while, "Delicious!" muffled by a mouthful. He had lost more weight, a pucker at the corner of each eye. We tore into our food, glad to have something to do, although I could barely swallow.

He rubbed his hands together, tugged at the short sleeves of his shirt. "When I'm out of here," he said, letting us get used to the feel of the words, emphasizing the phrase with his eyes, "When I'm out, I'm starting a service. For people who've bought cars that are defective."

Cindy said something I couldn't make out, busy with her Doritos. She cleared her throat and said, "You'd be proud of that Jaguar."

He thought about this, his chin jutted ironically, maybe wondering if he was, in fact, likely to feel proud of a car.

"It runs fine," Cindy said, and I could tell she was wounded by something that had passed between them. They had shared so little conversation in recent weeks that even a glance could hurt. It surprised me, the strength of her feelings.

"Consumers buy cars with cracked head gaskets," my father was saying, putting some kindness into his voice. "Faulty exhaust," he added, and Cindy smiled.

"Problems that don't show up when a mechanic peeks under the hood," Dad said. "I'll call it Lemonhounds, something like that. There's a huge market there."

The California State Bar Association had compensated my father's clients, and he could never practice law in the state again. Miss P told me that no one expected a competing diver to be able to handle pre-med classes.

Cindy was saying it was a good idea, she could picture the business cards, a lemon driving a car.

"A lemon in a car." Dad laughed, affectionately, too hard.

"A hound driving a lemon," I said.

His eyes brightened. "Good idea, Champion."

I could not look at him for a moment.

"I'm going to get it all back, Bonnie," he was saying, leaning toward me across the table. "All of it."

"We still have contacts, people who believe in Harvey," Cindy said. "They'll set Harvey up again like this." She snapped her fingers, softly, so it didn't make a sound.

When a guard called over a loudspeaker, "Visiting hours are over," the inmates began to stand up but didn't leave their stations.

Dad cocked his head in the direction of the PA system, a round hole covered with a steel grid up near the ceiling. He gave me a you-wouldn't-believe-this-place roll of his eyes, like this was a restaurant where the service was terrible. The food was bad, and they ignored you when you asked for your check.

I had come with so many things to say, that I still believed in him.

He said, "Next time, Champion."

Without anyone telling us, we made sure the chairs were pushed all the way in against the tables. The inmates lined up against the far wall, and the visitors lined up against the other. We began to leave the place, two lines walking in opposite directions, but ours was slower.

I watched as he filed from the room, laughing with one of the guards.

ABOUT MICHAEL CADNUM

I sit down to write every morning, and I don't know what will happen. I don't plan my novels in great detail. I have the feeling the world of my characters is waiting to be discovered, if I garden carefully enough, and clear away the weeds.

I think one of the things I love about reading is that it is a quietly joyful act, the writer and reader in a conspiracy together, a green secret, one that brings places and characters to life. A reader can carry his secret around with his lunch, or leave it at home in a special place, and it will be there, waiting. Sometimes in the middle of a hectic day I find myself quietly happy, filled with some unknown good news. And then I remember the book I have been reading, the secret waiting for me at home.

I live with my wife, Sherina, and when I look out of my window I see San Francisco across the bay.

Heat is my fourteenth novel. I have also written two books of poetry, many short stories, and a picture book for children, *The Lost and Found House* (Viking).